König was forcing his pocket battleship the *Kaiser Wilhelm* into a daring break-through for home, but as he neared the parallel of sixty north, he saw the *Constant*—and made his decision. . . .

His first thought that she was a harmless old merchantman proved to be a mistake. She was a cruiser, and although old and decrepit, he could not let her stand in his path. She must be destroyed. . . .

He gave the signal to fire—and the first salvo from his eleven-inch guns wrought shocking havoc on the decks of the *Constant*. But shaking off her hurt, the old cruiser moved sluggishly on, striking a course towards her distant foe.

The ultimate hour had arrived . . . König had already underestimated his enemy once—now he would have to crush her for good. . . .

And the *Constant* kept on—straight into a terrible onslaught from the *Kaiser*'s guns —for her there could be no retreat. . . .

KENNETH POOLMAN

TEACH 'EM TO DIE

CORGI BOOKS
TRANSWORLD PUBLISHERS LTD
A National General Company

TEACH 'EM TO DIE

A CORGI BOOK 552 07887 5

Originally published in Great Britain under
the title THE BATTLE OF SIXTY NORTH
by Cassell & Company, Ltd.

PRINTING HISTORY

Cassell Edition published 1958
Corgi Edition published 1959
Corgi Edition reissued 1968
Corgi Edition reprinted 1970
Corgi Edition reprinted 1970

This book is set in
Plantin 9/11 pt.

Corgi Books are published by Transworld Publishers, Ltd.,
Cavendish House, 57–59 Uxbridge Road, Ealing, London, W.5

Made and printed in Great Britain by
Richard Clay (The Chaucer Press), Ltd., Bungay, Suffolk

TEACH 'EM TO DIE

CHAPTER ONE

'AND the Lord said "Light", and there *was* light—and you could see for flamin' miles,' said the petty officer of the watch of H.M.S. *Constant* into the chin of his duffle coat. 'I wish He'd come and do something about this flamin' fog. I can't even see the oggin.'

'God knows how they'll find the ship,' said the bosun's mate, blowing on his hands.

'If it hadn't been for this bloody pea-souper we couldv'e gone alongside as per usual and the whole lot would be inboard by now,' grumbled the petty officer. He went to the rail near the top of the after gangway and stared hard into the grey pall which hid Rosyth like a smoke screen.

The acrid fog clothed them, swaddled them, hiding the grey water of the Firth of Forth and the forlorn wasteland of the docks which lay somewhere out there under the same cold, congealing shroud.

Somewhere out there also a small boat was lost, at that moment groping her way between the land and the ships swinging round their hooks in the stream. They swung slowly, battleships, carriers, cruisers, destroyers, with the imponderable slowness of planets in space, heavy and full of menace.

No one ship could see another. There was nothing to see but fog, nothing to taste but fog, nothing to fear but fog. For ships there is always fear when there is fog.

The voice of fog is a moaning siren. It calls and makes men on watch fearful and neurotically alert. It bays suddenly and wakes men sleeping to throbbing awareness. Fog is the stealthy noise in the room below that wakes you trembling. Fog is fear of danger and death, but even more it is fear of the unknown.

The *Constant* lay entomed within it now, hidden from all the other ships riding at anchor, silent and sullen. They were like great houses in the mist. The small boat wandered and stumbled, looking for a homely light.

The three men, petty officer, bosun's mate and side-boy, at *Constant*'s gangway, were joined by the officer of the day.

'Any sign of them, P.O.?' he asked, coming to the top of the gangway and standing with his hands on his hips, straining his eyes anxiously like the others into the heavy cloud an arm's length away.

'No, sir, not a sausage,' said the petty officer.

'Well, they should have been alongside twenty minutes ago according to the signal.' He was a young officer and the responsibility lay heavy upon him. The petty officer, twenty years his senior, knew this.

'They'll be here, sir,' he said, as reassuringly as he could without sounding familiar. Some of these young ninety-day wonders got a bit uppity if they thought you were trying to hold their hands.

'Lieutenant-Commander Dickinson wants to know as soon as they're sighted,' said the officer, then added impulsively, 'though I'm blessed if I know why anyone should *want* to turn out in this. . . .' He waved a hand vaguely at the fog and gave a nervous little giggle, conscious that he should not have given way to the expression of his thoughts. Won't you ever learn to keep your mouth shut, he thought angrily. Never be familiar with the men. Give them an inch and they'll take a mile.

The other man smiled inwardly, reading the young man's thoughts like the pages of the *Seamanship Manual*. All right, son. I know my place, don't worry. I won't take you up on it, I won't abuse the privilege of your silly confidence. He wanted to say, out loud: Old Dickinson doesn't *want* to come up here in the cold and filthy fag end of the second dog watch in bloody Rosyth, but he knows it's his duty to turn out and he thinks the new men will feel better for seeing their divisional officer at the gangway when they come aboard—and he probably wants to keep an eye on you as well! He wanted to tell the green young officer all this, but he just said, 'No, sir,' respectfully.

'Very good,' said the officer stiffly, reacting against his lapse of a moment before. 'Er, carry on.' He had learned at *King Alfred*, the training establishment for R.N.V.R. officers, that a rating said 'Aye, aye,' to an officer, but an officer always said 'Very good' in response to a man's report.

The thought of *King Alfred* at this lonely moment in the fog brought a rush of reassurance and confidence to the young man's heart. They had thought well of him at *King Alfred*. He had scored high marks in field training and signals. He'd cheated a bit in the navigation exam, but then he wasn't the only one—that crafty ex-policeman in front of him had cribbed his whole paper. And his seamanship was first-class too, the seamanship officer had said as much to him personally and his examination results agreed, especially the ship-handling practical in the river at Portslade. That had been quite a *tour de force* on his part. With sinking heart he had watched cadet after cadet make a hash of it. If they hadn't rammed the boat ahead when they tried to come alongside, they had rammed the one astern. If they got the rudder right they forgot to give the right wheel order, then forgot to take the rudder off again in their panic and swung right out again without touching anything at all, or vice versa. They went astern when they should have gone ahead, or said 'Hard-a-starboard!' instead of 'Hard-a-port!' One wretched man, an ex-Oxford lecturer, had obviously thought he was conning the *Campbeltown* into St. Nazaire, because he sent the sturdy and long-suffering bows of the little *Vicuna* smartly into the jetty at right angles with full speed on, while the seamanship officer stood by, arms folded, impartial, grim ... Another had caused the for'ard spring to wrap itself firmly round the propeller shaft, with the result that the small vessel drifted rapidly astern and rammed a landing-craft, awakening a sergeant of marines, who had had his head down therein, into vicious and obscene abuse of all temporary, acting, unpaid, half-hard, illegitimate, pants-wetting, would-be officers. And they deserved it all.

He smiled at the memory, thinking with a glow of satisfaction of what had happened when his turn had come round. Perhaps he had gained by comparison with the odious display of the others. Anyway, he hadn't put a foot or given an order wrong.

With the sureness and swagger of a crack fleet destroyer, *Vicuna* had steamed nonchalantly downstream, turned smartly to starboard and made a perfect approach, port side to, between two other vessels. With an equal nonchalance, masking a trembling heart, her temporary captain had rung down 'Stop engines' and handed over to the next poor wretch.

Yes, he could handle a ship, there was no doubt about that ... surely. Nervous, yes, but he had done it all the same. Seamanship—excellent. Power of command—very good. But his real pride lay elsewhere. He had been top of his division at gunnery, the best gunner in 'A' class, Nelson Division, H.M.S. *King Alfred*, and that was something to be proud of. For what use were the fighting ships of His Majesty's Navy without good gunners?

And now came the rub. Top of his division in gunnery, one of the best cadets in his class, and what had Their Lordships done with him? Posted him at once to a destroyer or a M.T.B., which was what he had asked for? Not a bit of it. This brilliant young officer had been sent to a training cruiser, to the very ship he himself had trained on as a cadet before he had gone to *King Alfred*! He was hurt. It really was a bit much, with a war to be won and a desperate need for outstanding young men like himself to lead the great drive to final victory. Not even an old destroyer-escort or a corvette, but an old, clapped-out training cruiser, based on Rosyth, mincing up and down the Forth with an occasional sniff at the lusty salt breeze blowing in from the North Sea and a disdainful shrug of her bony, ancient shoulders —an old maid, unwedded and virginal, for in her twenty-five years of sea-time she had never seen action, whose blood had long since cooled and in whom the desire to engage anything more lewd and potent than a wooden target in a practice shoot had died somewhere back in the sterile thirties. And he a gunner! Why, old Connie's guns were so old you couldn't see daylight down the barrels!

It was a crying shame. But, unfortunately, it was a fact. Here he was, officer of the day, with an awkward, if not ugly, situation on his hands—much worse than bringing the *Vicuna* alongside, because he was so alone this time and the business in hand so very very real and urgent. As officer of the day he was responsible for the entire ship, 5,000 tons and 500 men of her, and God alone knew what could happen in a fog like this.... And now the dratted boat with the new training class on board was late, probably adrift out there at the mercy of whatever predatory, blundering vessel might fall upon her. And, as if that were not quite enough to crack his brittle confidence, the new captain was expected to join the ship at some time during the watch. He hadn't bargained for it in the least, it was all so awkward and ugly and vague and uncertain. It wasn't the way life should have been at all. ... Supposing....

But his fearful thoughts were brought up sharp by a shout, a stifled, distant, long-drawn-out hail from the unknown heart of the fog.

'... What ship are you?' A mournful, siren-like sound. 'What ship are you?' The lonely voice hung flat, trapped in the fog like a whisper in a soundproof room, like a lost soul afloat forever on the black, lustreless waters.

'*Constant!*' came the petty officer's bellow from near his ear, making him jump and his heart beat faster.

'... coming alongside....' He heard the first words only of the formal phrase, then he was out of the ghostly unreal fog and clattering hurriedly down the iron steps of the ladder to the wardroom flat and Lieutenant-Commander Dickinson's cabin, where he could, he knew, be sure of a harsh reception if he were a second later than he should have been, or if he bungled his report.... Frantically he rehearsed the simple message. The harsh electric light beat at him like a third degree spotlight.

He was outside the door. He gulped, his heart beating wildly. He raised his hand. He knocked.

'Yes?' came the gruff voice instantly. 'Come in.'

He stepped inside. 'Um....' *You fool, get it out!*

'Well?' The voice coming from that tall, grim figure was almost metallic. It had all the fear and chill stridence of the sirens that ground out their warning up there in the fog.

'The ... boat ... is coming alongside, sir, with the new class.' He shut his mouth thankfully and relaxed.

'I should think it's about had time to reach the gangway by

now,' said Dickinson tonelessly. He rose to his feet and reached for his cap; tall, big-boned and hard, grey in tone, grey in the lines of his face, grey in the empty bleakness of his eyes, iron grey at the temples, bleak and hard in voice and feature.

Dickinson led the way up into the outer world of dank fog, with the sub-lieutenant close on his heels, biting his lip, apprehensive. Up on deck, the lieutenant-commander went with long strides straight over to the rail and stood there, hands clasped behind his back, staring down at the launch packed tight with sailors. All wore stiff-looking matelots' caps set straight on their heads, ordinary naval issue greatcoats with the webbing strap of a gas-mask case across each chest making them all look as if there had recently been a mass award of some wartime, *ersatz* legion of honour. All wore some variation of mittens or gloves, navy-blue wool or leather, all looked sick and blue with the bitter cold of the fogbound November night. Most were sick with apprehension, too, and some, a miserable, shamefaced few, had succumbed, even at this early stage in their career as sailors, to the uneasy motion of the launch, which had been roaming the fog for some forty-five minutes before the man in the bows had spotted the bulk of *Constant*'s stern, a lighter grey patch in the greyness that surrounded them.

Dickinson watched them and no one could have guessed his thoughts. He did pity them for a brief moment. They did look, all of them, wretchedly miserable and cowed. He would have been surprised, even a little hurt, for there was somewhere still some fatherly kindness left in him, if he had been told at that moment that he, so grim and inflexible looming there in the mist like the very figurehead of all their fears, contributed to their misery. But for a fleeting moment he pitied them. Then his mood veered to gloom and bitterness again when he overheard his petty officer of the watch muttering, 'This lot looks worse than ever. Officers? Gawd 'elp England!'

Some would be more intelligent, some less; some would have the makings of character, though never enough, he thought, to meet his own and the Royal Navy's high standards; some would be strong, as strong as civilian sailors could be expected to be, some not strong enough. Those whose names, after four hard, testing weeks aboard *Constant* under his stern authority, he could write down on the credit side of his report as possessing some wartime imitation of officer-like qualities would go on to H.M.S. *King Alfred* at Brighton for further training before they became temporary officers of the Royal Naval Volunteer Reserve, holding the King's Commission and allegedly ready for general service with the Fleet. Regulars like himself had been viciously whittled down by four years of war. My Lords made constant demands for temporary officers and it was his job to maintain the supply.

Those who did not fit the pattern would mostly go to the naval depots at Chatham, Portsmouth or Devonport as ordinary seamen to await drafts to ships at home or abroad. All of them, passed or failed, he knew, would be glad to leave the *Constant*, to them a kind of hell ship, and the 'lucky' few who were borderline cases to be given a 're-scrub' or another four weeks aboard the ship, would be the most wretchedly cast down of all, although it was the ones who had been rejected who would suffer most, did they but know it, when they reached barracks. Not many regular Royal Naval officers knew anything about the life of men in Royal Naval barracks in wartime, but Dickinson knew. He knew a great deal more than any of his men suspected about the hardness of lower deck life. He knew all about the squalor of barracks, of H.M.S. *Pembroke* at Chatham, that grim pile, half prison, half workhouse, which without accommodation for more than a fraction of the men quartered there, without washing or sanitary arrangements other than the most primitive, without any relieving decency at all, gave a few tuberculosis and their ticket out of the Navy and broke the young heart of many a mother's son, turning all but the minority of stubborn rebels into sycophants for cushy numbers in the drafting office or depot school, into petty officers' toadies or barrack guard boot-lickers. Dickinson knew all about conditions in barracks. He knew it because once upon a time there had been a mutiny against these conditions, a small but significant one, in a Royal Naval barracks, and he, with fixed bayonets at his back, had been orderd to suppress it. He had done his duty, knowing beyond all doubt that it was his duty, but at the end of a brutal and bloody half-hour a young man lay dead from a bayonet thrust through the stomach. When he failed a boy now and sent him to R.N.B. he knew better than anyone what he was sending him to. But he did his duty, knowing beyond all doubt, and hating it, that it was his duty.

Dickinson, tall, grey and lonely, stood apart there on the quarterdeck and watched the blur of white faces under their dark blue, pusser's issue caps.

Pity? Yes, he felt pity, but most of it was for himself. Like a corrosive, yellow acid, it bit into his soul. Any feelings he had for these wretched, aspiring, stupidly ambitious boys down there in the tossing boat, so uneasy and so miserable on the threshold of that life of trouble and pain and responsibility which he himself had trod for so long, any finer strain of tolerance or affection which might still be there, buried deep, was thrust deeper still by the great stone weight of sorrow, bitterness and hopeless, impotent anger which lay over him, dark and heavy as the fog, and which the sight of all these young faces had brought back once more in full black flood.

For the boys themselves in the boat, the officer candidates, it was a frightening and fearful scene. The fog and the heaving launch, the strange, grim shape of the ship stretching into the blackness made it much worse than, say, joining a new school. To them *Constant* looked rather like a great floating prison or an institution. They themselves felt, deeply and uneasily, something like convicts passing through the prison gates.

It was early yet for them to know the full misery of the draftee and to recognise the pain of this kind of exile for what it was. But they had had one sharp taste of it when the tumbril of the drafting lorry had dragged them inexorably away from the training depot, and when they had spent a few unpleasant days and nights in barracks on transit to the *Constant*. At the training depot, for all its humiliations and terrors, its boredom and bull, they had managed after a few weeks to establish a sort of uneasy substitute for home life. The camaraderie of conscripts together in an eternity of hard labour; the grim and delicious humour of the old long-service instructors; the shy encounters with Wrens at music concerts and ship's dances; the occasional runs ashore for dinner at the White Horse in Ipswich, all this had come to form a basis of a sort of stability, the vague framework of a way of life abruptly shattered when suddenly the eight weeks of training ran out and they found themselves for the first time on draft.

As they lined up then in the cold grey dawn waiting for the draft lorries to take them to the station, they looked for the last time at H.M.S. *Ganges* and saw it as an infinitely friendly place, a home, a place of a thousand warm and intimate associations from which they were being torn by the unfeeling, calloused hands of the Navy.

The great gritty parade ground, wet and forlorn in the drizzle that wept upon them, stretched from the three-decker's mast in front of them away across boot-churned acres to the chief and petty officers' mess, dimly seen through the rain at the far end.

Ordinary Seaman Wilsher remembered the chief and petty officers' mess and would remember it always. He would remember particularly the flower beds in front of it, for he had once sent a squad marching off down the parade ground until they were out of earshot and deaf to his desperate, stuttered commands, marching on for ever like three blue ranks of sorcerer's broomsticks right through those flower beds....

Ordinary Seaman Moore looked up at the towering mast, thick as a telephone box, and wondered how he could ever have been afraid of it. Once he had clung, utterly terrified, to those ratlines, at the point where they swung out sharply back over your head so that you had to cling on upside down like a fly and work your way out to the edge of the platform and hoist yourself over the elbow by the brass rail, trembling, grabbing at anything you could clutch. He remembered, wonderingly, that awful second when he had clung there, shaking violently, heart pumping, under the overhang, until fear gave way to shame and shame to blind anger so that he swarmed up and over like an ape or a soldier thrusting his weak and shameful body over the top ... then standing up tall and confident on the platform, looking disdainfully at the poor wretch whose nerve really had gone and who crawled now miserably up through the lubber's hole. It was just a breathless athletic exercise after that, a stark symbol for achievement, like mountain climbing. Almost contemptuously he had gone up to the second crosstrees, swung up and over, across and down again, hanging by his hands alone until his boots found the rungs of the ratlines slanting away beneath him. As he looked up at that towering and once terrible height he felt fondness for it, and gratitude. Nobody knew, nobody could know what that little victory had meant to him.

Ordinary Seaman McCutchen looked at it too, but it meant something very different to him. McCutchen was the one who had gone up through the lubber's hole. To him the great mast was a thing of shame and panic. Once that great, grim tower, symbol of strength, symbol of iron manhood, had swayed with all its great spars and sails through lashing gales and jazzing tropic air, holding firm, iron men in a wooden ship, with the massive fortitude of the Royal Navy, keeping station through half a century of grey weather. Often McCutchen dreamed himself aloft on this terrible mast, rolling in drunken parabolas round a nightmare sky, for ever about to fall down, down into that dark, howling sea, hanging, slipping, screaming.... The real mast did not roll now, its old step fixed in a petrified sea of concrete and asphalt, but the nightmare was no nightmare when he hung, livid and shaking with panic at the bottom of the elbow, with those terrible ratlines soaring outwards over his head.... He couldn't do it, he couldn't do it, but had to go straight up and through the lubber's hole.

McCutchen could hardly believe that this miserable coward was himself. He had thought himself a tough, down-to-earth, no-nonsense chap among these wet, namby-pamby college boys. But the namby-pambies climbed the elbow and tough, down-to-earth, no-nonsense Jack McCutchen funked it and went up through the lubber's hole. If you were going to be an officer you had to do all that a sailor did and a bit more before you proved yourself worthy. The instructor hadn't been looking during those two minutes when McCutchen was a coward. Now McCutchen wanted desperately to become an officer, to prove himself, to banish that ugly cadaver of fear which lay buried within him.

The *Constant* had a mast, of course, but he didn't think it was a thing you had to climb, just a pole for wireless aerials. It would be all classroom staff there, he was sure, there would be no swaying tower to climb, no nightmares. The need for iron men had passed with the wooden ships....

He *had* to pass, he *had* to, he could not fail. He tried to drug himself in this way, to hypnotise mind and will, screwing his ailing resolution to the sticking point. I will pass, I will pass, he told himself a thousand times a day, a self-imposed faith healer fearfully suspecting quackery. But now he knew he could fail. For the first time, with wonder as well as fear, he had seen failure face to face, heard its whisper, smelled its corruption, and the world had shrunk from the great golden land of luck it had once seemed. That golden land he knew was a mirage, its easy promise gone for ever. But still he told himself *I will pass, I will pass,* still in the dream of all-powerful adolescence. Still *I will get there, I will reach that vision and the way will always be easy and I'll always be happy,* his troubled heart muttered desperately.

Now, in the heaving boat under the cruiser's looming stern, cold, stale, tired and apprehensive of the future, he, and anyone else there who sheltered similar fears, forgot them for the moment. Now if they feared anything definite at all it was for their very survival on this monstrous, cold iron ship breathing fog and fear like a great scaly dragon lying half awake on the water. In their loneliness and fear of the future the cruiser was more than a ship to them. It was a huge, megalithic monster with stony, baleful eyes—the Royal Navy, the monster that had snatched them away from the easy, swaddling life of home and pubs and girls.

No one in the boat could have expressed their fears thus vividly, except perhaps Moore. Moore looked fragile, because he was slim and had long delicate fingers and soft brown eyes. But Moore was in many ways immune from life's harshness. Moore was a poet. He was being a poet now, here in the launch in the fog, not a sailor at all—that curious, bizarre and fascinating person had his head down, taking a brief stand-easy in the back of Moore's chameleon-coloured mind. The whole darkness and harshness of the environment made by contrast lamps burn in his brain, golden firelight flicker there in the lithe shapes of images. Every statement implies its opposite, action and reaction are opposite and equal—it is the law of creation. *What golden things does fog hide, what paradise?* said his mind, creating rhythmic runs of words like glowing spurts of molten metal, *What songs, what loves, what wild surprise, hanging like Christmas beyond the night? Dying things? Dreams? Longings that moan but whether near or far all unknown, like white gulls lost between day and darkness?* He was unassailable now, immune. In the argot of matelots he was inboard, he was fireproof. Objects did not exist for him—mere *things,* the boat, the sea, the fog and the fear that were all one and the same, the 5,000 hard, wet, barnacled, paint-daubed tons of the cruiser, these *things* had no reality beyond vaguely sensed phenomena like stage props stored away in that strange ship's chandler's caboosh where the sometime-living, hornpiping Jack-my-Hearty sailor slept. *Or is the dawn alive behind this doom? Shall we strike clear and make our landfall soon—beyond the moaning siren of our fear?*

When he felt like this he had no fear of war, of death by all the ways in which mere things can kill, of cruisers and guns and collisions in the fog, nor of failure to succeed and make his mark in the world. Poet and sailor wrestled within him always, for he loved things for their own sake as well, the things in that small bizarre back room, naked, stark lovely things that shocked the senses, food and drink and women and beautiful things. All these the sailor loved, the wanderer for ever in love with the lights of home jazzing in the water. But it was something else the poet loved, a world underneath the water, behind the fog, beyond a girl's smile or an apple's cold kiss. He stared at the cruiser's great cold shape, and felt somehow that the poet was already aboard and getting fat on pusser's grub and rum, but that the sailor whose navy blue he wore would never reach home or harbour, would die slowly, drowning, an eternal survivor grasping at real life. *What golden things does fog hide, what paradise? What songs, what loves, what wild surprise, hanging like Christmas beyond the night?* The poet spoke for all the sailors around him, his own sailor lost and stumbling in the fog.

Then the jar and bump of the boat against 5,000 tons of heavy, imponderable steel shocked the dozing sailor awake. The light went out, the fog gathered and the cold and ordinary fear struck him. What will happen to me? was his only thought. How will I fend off all this bloody misery and be an officer and live soft again? Then he looked up and saw the tall figure of the lieutenant-commander standing on the cruiser's deck. His heart quailed. Here was Authority, iron-willed and despotic, cruel and cold. It would stamp on his silly poetry, sail his small cockleshell under. The tall grey figure loomed, one with the rock-like face of the great grey ship, a swirl of fog wreathing his head, breathing and glaring fear and coldness.

Dickinson picked out the slim youth, mooning out across the water, and stared at him as if he knew him—the eternal helpless, hopeless, hapless civilian sailor boy, the kind they sent to him regularly, once a week, twenty at a time, in a bewildered bundle. What will happen when all the old professionals like me have been killed off—and God knows there aren't many of us left? Can these boys fight a war at sea? Can that youth there looking so sick and frightened withstand the terrible things I've seen, the awful ways in which even hardened, experienced seamen can be tested and hurt and found wanting?

Deep in these heavy-hearted thoughts he returned below. There, staring and smiling at him from their leather frames—the kind that fold up and stow in the pocket, the ones that she had bought him the day before he went to sea in August 1939—were their faces again, and all that agony, touched off by his other fears and doubts, burst in him. Grey with misery he stared at them. He reached out a hand, prompted by a sudden stab of reason, to pick them up and put them in a drawer somewhere. But he held back, as he always did. What good would that do? What use to hide them in a drawer when their images would light his mind and eat at his heart for ever? Better to let them stay out in the harsh electric daylight, the light he never switched off, because the dark and the sleeplessness were too terrible to face. . . .

The sudden knock at the cabin door came like a thunderclap. He started and his heart pounded.

'Yes?'

A startled young face appeared round the door. It was that conceited young idiot of a subby again.

'S . . . s . . . sir!' the young officer spluttered. 'Sir, the . . . um . . . the, um, the captain is coming alongside, sir.'

Dickinson nodded. Here we go again. I wonder what they've sent us this time.

CHAPTER TWO

DAWN crept over the water like the trilling of a bosun's pipe. Sunrise came out of the east like a bugle call.

The fog had dispersed in the night. By the end of the middle watch at four o'clock the sky was bare and cold and all the stars of spring glittered there. By first light the last feathery wisp of mist had vanished from the hills. The sun rising out of the North Sea sparkled along the Forth like firelight on a new-forged blade and touched the cold hills to purple and russet and gold.

Wherever the awakening sunshine stumbled on a ship there was a gap in the path of light, a patch of shadow in her lee. In this chilly penumbra boats shuffled drowsily to the humming of the tide, their painters pulling at the white lizards which kept them fast to the ships' booms like drowsy puppies.

The training cruiser swung slowly round her anchor, her ensign lifting and stirring in the light breeze of morning. There was no sign of life aboard her, for the quartermaster and side-boy, the only men on deck, were snug in their caboosh on the quarterdeck, yawning and scratching themselves, feeling stale and dirty.

'Roll on my twelve!' said the quartermaster of *Constant*.

'Roll on my breakfast!' said the side-boy, a cadet.

'That won't do a growing lad much good any road,' said the quartermaster, an elderly stripey with a greasy cap pushed down over his low forehead and an enormous greatcoat swaddling him from head to toe. 'Herrings-in again, I 'spect.' He broke wind loudly. 'Stick.' He broke wind again. 'Bust.' He stretched and figured the bosun's pipe which hung by a silver chain round his neck. 'Oh well, time to call the 'ands.' He lumbered to his feet, stuck his head out into the morning air and broke wind for the third time. 'Off to the moon.' He disappeared from view and a minute later the shivering cadet heard the shrill bleat of the pipe and the old matelot's distant raucous bellow as he greeted the shy virgin dawn with: 'Wakey, wakey! Heave-o, heave-o, heave-o, lash up and stow, the morning's fine, the sun's burning yer bleedin' eyes out!'

An hour later, with roughly one and a half herrings-in-tomato lying uneasily and clammily upon each quivering stomach, the cadets fell in, each division to a separate part of the ship, first-week cadets to the foretop division in the waist of the ship to port, second-week cadets on the opposite side in maintop division, third-weekers aft on the quarterdeck and the swells, the sixth form, the fourth-week men, up on the fo'c'sle in two lines of navy blue.

Each cadet had a white, or off-white, arm band with a number lashed round his left arm. All were in ordinary matelot's square rig but wore their caps dead centre with clumsy, badly tied bows on the left-hand side, strictly in accordance with regulations. This, and their ill-fitting issue uniforms, distinguished cadet ratings from real sailors, who would rather be seen dead than appear in public without the huge, neatly sewn butterfly of an 'eye-shooting' bow bang in the front of the cap between the eyes; without skin-tight jumper silver-zipped down the sides and button cuffs; wide bell-bottoms with carefully ironed concertina creases horizontally up the legs, and such flamboyant fripperies as pusser's black slippers with silver buckles, collars bleached almost white and knee-length tapes.

Cadet ratings had none of these marks of naval *haute couture*, nor did they dare to go in for so much as a tiddley bow or a burberry in place of a regulation greatcoat. And they must not say, 'Got a glim, wings?' but 'May I trouble you for a light, old chap?'

They were all, as they stood fallen in in the chill of a Scottish dawn, in various degrees of wretchedness, ranging from the just-joined to the old salts who had now done three weeks sea-time and had only one week more to go. It was a state of mind which the more experienced fourth-weekers had learned to call 'chokka to the eyebrows'.

When the cruiser weighed, only the senior class on the fo'c'sle was busy, for they, under the supervision of their divisional officer and a veteran petty officer, had the job of heaving in the anchor. In fact, of course, the donkey engine did the heaving. The cadets washed the mud off the anchor and cable with a hose as it came up through the navel pipe, handled the flags which told the captain on the bridge how much cable had been run out or hauled in, put on the Blake slips and bottle-screw slips which held cable and anchor firm once it was inboard and generally squared things off on the fo'c'sle. It was a practical lesson in anchors and cables, a demonstration which they ought to have been marking, leaning and inwardly digesting. But most of them were too cold and hungry and chokka, and too pre-occupied in digesting those filthy herrings-in, to care.

'Little beggars!' thought the petty officer in disgust.

'Couldn't care less. All they think of is getting a gold ring on their arm and a bit of crumpet in a taxi. Then one day they'll find themselves fo'c'sle officers and some poor old beggar like me'll have to hold their hands and do their job for 'em!'

The *Constant* turned slowly out into the main stream and steamed on down the Forth, making for May Island and the sea. She was an old ship, but to a watcher on the russet hills she would have made a lovely and a graceful spectacle as she glided through the grey satin sheen of the water, pushing pearls before her at her bows.

She was the oldest cruiser in the Navy, a page from cruiser history.

In the year before the First World War broke out the Royal Navy had begun to design and build a new type of light cruiser to meet modern needs. These were for a ship with enough speed, manoeuvrability and gunpower to protect our torpedo-boat destroyers and to sink enemy ones, to scout ahead of the battle fleet, and to protect our merchant ships against fast raiding cruisers.

With the advent of oil fuel for the propulsion of ships they were able to do this. Coal had put a limit on the size of light cruisers, but now they were able to revert to a smaller tonnage and still have the speed they wanted.

They built a ship of 3,000 tons, the lovely *Arethusa,* and used her as a basis for a fresh departure. They made many variations upon the theme, mainly in guns. The first new cruisers had two big six-inch guns and a cluster of small four-inch.

Then came the war. The Battle of Heligoland Bight in 1914 and other encounters tested these early experiments severely. The six-inch guns were proved very good for the job, the four-inch useless, so these pop-guns were ripped out of all the other cruisers which had been built or were being completed on similar lines and only six-inch fitted.

A ship with lovely, rakish lines and a simple, easily controlled armament of four six-inch guns, all mounted on the centre line of the ship, was the result. These ships were good but they could have been better, for they had quality at the expense of quantity in gunpower. The *Constant* was one of these under-gunned, though beautiful ships. Later the Admiralty designers copied the new 'dreadnought' battleships of the *Iron Duke* class and arranged two extra six-inch guns to fire over the top of the old single ones on the fo'c'sle and on the quarterdeck. They then had the perfect gun platform, and the light cruiser has remained basically the same ever since. The *Constant* missed all this fine flower of cruiser development, and when in the thirties they put the six-inch in pairs in turrets and built round them the beautiful *Leanders* the old ship looked like a museum piece.

Constant was built on the River Tyne. Her launch was delayed by a fire on board and she never felt the wind of war in her rigging. To make her pique more acute the improved 'dreadnought' version, the *Coventry* class, completely outshone her even before she had felt the kiss of salt water and sniffed the heady scent of the oceans she had been built to guard.

It was a shame that her sudden wooing, when she was considered past hope, had turned out such a flop after all. The old ship was like an elderly virgin who finds herself wanted at last—but not for her beauty. When she was selected to train cadets it seemed to rub in the bitter truth that she could never inspire passion, for war had twice passed her by without a second look.

It was therefore fitting in every way that she should have become a floating classroom.

As such, *Constant* was a daring experiment. When war broke out all would-be officers of the Royal Naval Volunteer Reserve had to spend several months at sea in an operational ship of war before they could be considered as candidates for the King's Commission, and go to a shore establishment for further training. It was not very long, however, before the Admiralty found that this method of selection did not produce enough officers to man the expanding Fleet. Sea-time for officer-cadets must be cut down and properly regularised and organised so that large batches of suitable new entries could be trained rapidly and commissioned as officers to augment the previous rather haphazard scheme.

The obvious answer was a sea-going training ship. She would have to be an operational type of vessel, similar to the sort of ship the cadets would be drafted to when they became officers, but, on the other hand, the shortage of any kind of operational ship was so acute that the Board of Admiralty was reluctant to spare any.

Bitterly they thought of those ships scrapped in the wishful days of disarmament before the war. The Navy could have done with every one of them now. The few which had been retained were every day proving themselves potent veterans, old but still fighting fit. None could be released for training duties.

But there was one ship, a Great War relic miraculously preserved, which might be spared. She was still fit for sea, although she was too decrepit to send out against the enemy. This old ship had in fact actually beeen consigned to scrap just after Munich, when the promise of 'peace in our time' seemed to destroy any excuse for keeping her on strength. When war seemed inevitable at last, however, in the spring of 1939, she was reprieved. The old vessel had actually arrived at Battleship Yard in Blyth, Northumberland, to be broken up, when the order came to save her and refit her for use.

By that time she had already lain for several days alongside the grey wharf, awaiting her turn to be broken up. Her shafts had stopped turning in their oily tunnels; her pistons, once so supple and willing, were still now in the first stages of *rigor mortis*, and all the life had left her. She was a grey hulk.

Berthed ahead of her was the rusty relic of a ship already in the last stages of destruction. Great broken ribs stuck out between rusty plates, huge chasms yawned above her ruptured 'tween-decks and everywhere the cold, pitiless blue flames of the oxy-acetylene torches ate into iron and steel. She was a carcass rummaged by the vultures of the cranes. Astern of this broken and dismembered ship, the old cruiser awaited her turn to share the same fate, and from being a taut, trim, lovely vessel to become rusty steel scrap for the factories to turn into peaceful things like ploughs and pen nibs, motor-cars and machinery for industry, and her polished woodwork to be fashioned into garden furniture for old ladies and gentlemen to sit on in the long drowsy twilight of their once-active lives.

Across the water from the cruiser's last berth another carcass, red with rust, lay helpless under the cranes. At a quick glance you might have imagined that here was another victim, half dismembered. In fact she was half built, a fledgling ship. The rust which covered her plating came from long hours at her building berth under the rainy northern skies. She was a fine new destroyer in the making and all that seeming decay would soon disappear under the fiery red-lead and the first cool, pale grey paint.

The *Constant* had looked like that once, poised on a Tyneside slipway waiting for the crystal champagne kiss and the blessing which sent her gliding proudly down into the coaly river. Now she was old, and without her guns looked like a toothless old maid.

But in the month of August, when Hitler seemed about to strike, every available ship of the Royal Navy was mobilised and sent to sea. An urgent message came through to the general manager at Battleship Yard and he received a visit from a senior naval officer who came up from Newcastle upon Tyne with a big new contract for the firm whose business had been to destroy ships.

They would destroy no more ships for many years to come. From now on they would build and fit out ships, and they would begin right away—with the *Constant.*

That very morning the last remaining bottom plates and keel of the previous job had been towed away to the tidal dock for final destruction, and the big cranes had swung their lowering gantries over the cruiser. . . . But the first thing those cranes did now was to lift the guns which had so recently been taken out of her back into her again, filling the ugly, gaping sockets where they had been. And very soon the pistons began to limber into their supple stride again, the idle shafts turning slowly in their oily tunnels like sleeping giants awakening, the life returning to the cold metal with a rustle and a sigh like a woman dressing for her lover.

It was unquestionably a good idea to use her to train young officers. Before she could begin her new job, however, she had to be refitted extensively, mainly to find the space for classrooms amidships, where the cadets would be taught the theoretical seamanship, gunnery, navigation and ship handling which they would have ample chance of putting into hard practice without moving more than a heaving line's distance—though it would be *very* hard practice and they would be moving to it on the double.

In fact the whole scheme would have to be rushed through. The C.W. branch of the R.N.V.R., in its frowsty warren at Queen Anne's Mansions in London, whose job it was to make the bright idea work, brought out a tentative syllabus combining theoretical and practical work to cover a period of four weeks' training aboard the cruiser. Each week there was to be a fresh intake of twenty trainees, all of whom would come to the *Constant* straight from one of the big primary training depots for new entries, where they would have been previously selected as potential officer material.

This meant that they would be very green to start with, and four weeks at sea in a non-operational ship would have to be four very full weeks indeed if they were to arrive at the final testing ground of H.M.S. *King Alfred* at Brighton with more than the knowledge of which was the blunt end and which was the sharp.

First and foremost, their instructors would have to be strict disciplinarians. Some of these would of course be R.N.V.R. officers themselves. That was only common sense. But the Admiralty thought it vital that the basic character of the training should be very firmly 'R.N.', with a predominance of professional, Dartmouth-trained and experienced officers to head the executive departments of the ship herself and double with the duties of divisional officers and instructors for the cadets. The chief and petty officer instructors and ship's company, it was thought, could very well be old, experienced seamen of the regular Navy, who would be able to pass on the spirit and outlook of the Service without tending to be unduly sympathetic to the raw material just because it was ex-civilian.

The net result was that the *Constant*, spick and span and Blyth-fashion in new paint, was commissioned by a crew of veterans, pensioners and hard cases, with a few ex-civilian officers dotted here and there. The officers although picked for their efficiency as seamen and their devotion to duty, were mostly men whom the Service and the war had treated indifferently, if not harshly, and this treatment was reflected in their handling of the first cadets. The non-commissioned instructors and the leading hands in charge of messes were all men who had seen a lot of war and hard sea-time, the younger ones in the floating labour exchanges of the peacetime Navy and in the early days of Hitler's war; the older men, of whom there was a predominance, in the First World War and the years immediately after. Some of these were pensioners recalled to the Service in August, 1939, from civilian life, where they had been keeping little shops or pubs or simply cultivating their allotments. Of these veterans, those who had been happy in their retirement mostly hated the sudden brutal uprooting from the soil of a long-awaited, well-deserved haven ashore to the bleak and brassy life of bull they thought they had left for ever. Those who had found civvy street a cold and alien thoroughfare now had a grudge against the world and were not likely to treat the sons of middle-class professional men with conspicuous kindness.

So *Constant* had the makings of what a soft civilian would call a hell-ship from the start. She was what the Service knows as a 'pusser' ship—spit and polish, strict discipline and no excuse for shirking. This was the new home for the boys from the secondary and public schools who thought they wanted to be naval officers. So they want to be officers and gentlemen, do they? All right, they've asked for it!

By the winter of 1941–2 the training scheme had been in operation for some months and had had a chance to prove itself. In the early stages it had almost foundered. Conditions had been so harsh that a month of them had produced a pack of bloody-minded skates and shirkers whose first aim was to find a hole in the ground or a cushy number in barracks and *never, never* go to sea again. Only the hard core, the lads with real character, had survived and become officers, and even they looked back on the *Constant* with hatred.

But there were changes. Slowly the scroungers and jankers men, the sour and stupid martinets, all that flotsam which commanding officers of fighting ships had been glad to foist on the training branch when the call had gone out for 'suitable' volunteers to make up *Constant*'s ship's company, gradually all these were weeded out. A better type replaced them, for the Navy began to realise that only the best were good enough to provide the intensive training, in character as well as in seamanship, necessary to turn civilians into naval officers. So many of the best, of course, were dead, gone with all the splendid ships which Hitler's ships and bombers had smashed. But the Admiralty took some of the tired veterans who were left and sent them to the *Constant*. It was a rest cure for them and they were able to pass on some of the fighting spirit and fine seamanship which had held off the Germans to the young men who were to take up the torch from them.

To these veterans the young cadets seemed like babes in arms. They themselves had seen and suffered so much, they had been exposed so long to the worst furies of war at sea, they had watched so many even of the strongest and bravest and most experienced professional sailors wither in the hot breath of the blitzkrieg, that they believed this savage war too terrible for mere schoolboys to face.

They were so utterly vulnerable and inexperienced, these

boys. Of the sailor's trade they knew nothing. But that was relatively unimportant—they were the pick of the bunch after all, the cream of the new entries, and they could be taught.

But what of the other things? What of the boundless patience and resolve, the deep reserves of bodily stamina and mental toughness demanded by endless, red-eyed hours on watch in charge of a priceless warship and her men, a grim vigil apt to be broken abruptly by the jangling call to action and the need to stay cool, to make the right decision in a split second? What of the rare maturity and integrity that a man must possess to withstand all these aching hardships and dangers and responsibilities, and conquer all their urgent and endless demands? Could all this be taught in the classroom of an old training cruiser, chunking round and round May Island in the Firth of Forth, with an occasional half-hearted cruise for a few miles up the coast, to do night exercise of a practice shoot with a bored destroyer?

They were boys, when the crises demanded men. To make matters worse, the opening of this black year of 1942 saw Britain and her allies in graver peril and under far greater strain than ever before. On land all the allied armies were locked in a desperate, backs-to-the-wall struggle with the armies of the Axis. On the sea they were in even worse straits.

In the Mediterranean, after the brief comparative lull when the Luftwaffe had withdrawn from its Sicilian airfields to throw its weight into the attack on Russia, our depleted Fleet faced the renewal of the attack by Kesselring's massed bombers at a time when we had little or no air cover over our ships, for most of our carriers were sunk or under repair in American yards. In the Atlantic, the U-boat wolf packs were mounting a crushing blitz on our merchantmen and their under-strength, overworked escorts, and the rate of sinkings was increasing alarmingly. In the east the day was darkest of all. The Japanese had just crashed into the war and so shattered the Allied naval squadrons there that they now had command of the seas from Midway in the Pacific to Addu Atoll, west of Ceylon, where a scratch British squadron calling itself the 'Eastern Fleet' had been forced to hide to keep its puny strength 'in being'.

This was the war the Royal Navy faced. Everywhere, all over the oceans of the world, its men were being killed by a ruthless, highly skilled enemy. At home the shipyards were turning out ships as fast as they could.

To replace these fallen men, to man the new carriers, cruisers, destroyers and escort vessels, many more young men from homes and schools in Britain and the Commonwealth would be needed. Above all, the demand would be for officers to lead the men and steer the ships towards the tiny lamp of hope which flickered low on the faraway, dark horizon across a grey waste of sea.

The Navy would need many more men than *Constant* could send her, many more than the additional trickle which came from the messdecks of all the active service ships—and many promising officer candidates had been killed in these ships since 1939. In the early weeks of 1942, with the full tide of war once more rushing upon them, the Admiralty were already thinking seriously of stepping up the officer training programme.

There was no way of shortening the preliminary sea training of R.N.V.R. cadets any further. The only answer was to increase the numbers by stepping up the facilities for training. This meant more training ships. By now some of the cruisers slightly less aged than the *Constant* which had fought and survived this war so far had come to the end of their active service, worn out and driven to the limits of their old machinery, their trembling plates and palsied rivets. Two or three of these ships could be taken over and modified after the model of the *Constant*.

But before they would take this step, the Admiralty, cautious in all things, felt that they must be completely sure of the wisdom of it. Although the training seemed sound enough on paper, considering the short period given at sea, My Lords were still not convinced that the present scheme produced a man with the sort of character they looked for. After all, My Lords were all veterans too, all professionals to a man, and still had serious doubts that the young amateurs whom *Constant* mothered on them were up to their heavy responsibility.

In order to make sure they sent specially selected, highly

experienced officers to check up on the training scheme at all its stages.

As part of this process they appointed a new captain to H.M.S. *Constant*, who thus came to the old cruiser and her crew of callow youths and tired veterans as a sort of Inspector-General.

CHAPTER THREE

COMMANDER ALASTAIR ST. JOHN HARKER, D.S.O, D.S.C., R.N., thirty-three years old, was a veteran, a survivor like all the other regular officers and men who had been doing most of the fighting at sea. In Harker's case this was literally true, for he had just come from a destroyer which had been blown in two by a German dive-bomber off Crete. Harker, a lieutenant-commander then, was the only man to escape alive. There would have been more, but the German fighters which had homed on the scene of the kill like sharks on a blood scent, had come down and machine-gunned the handful of half-dead men struggling and choking in the black oil fuel. Harker, past all hope, had watched all his friends and shipmates die and had wanted to die himself in his black grief and despair. But he did not die. Exposure could not kill him, neither heat nor cold. Harker, like his new command, was a veteran, but he was a young one.

He was a small-ship man, heart and soul, through and through. Not for his fiery soul the gas and gaiters of battleships and carriers and cruisers, where bugles told a man when to eat and sleep and lick the Admiral's boots, where life was a thing of starch and stiff collars, of privilege and protocol. He was a bit of a buccaneer, like all small-ship sailors: freedom of the sea was his very breath. He hated four walls and formal gardens and rules made by men too much in love with a sterile security. He loathed snobs and armchair strategists. As for ships, he liked to use one as he would a fast car or a horse, to have them under his hand, to be directly in touch with every fibre of their fiery potent natures.

He therefore loved small ships and destroyers in particular. Whenever he heard a matelot say, 'Small ships, meself,' he knew him for the right sort.

'I'm a destroyer man,' he said with a grin to Dickinson, twelve years his senior. 'If I'd been given this ship in the Kaiser's war she might have been a bit more to my fancy. You'd never think to look at her now that she was designed to mix it with the boats—a destroyer of destroyers in fact.'

'She could still hold her own with a V and W,' said the older man, surprised at his sudden feeling of loyalty to the ship.

'God help her if she ever runs into anything bigger than that!' said Harker.

'She's still a good ship, sir,' argued Dickinson stiffly. 'Even,' he went on, a small wry smile on his lips, 'though I did overhear one of the cadets saying that you couldn't see daylight down the barrels of the six-inch. Of course, we've got no radar.'

'That's being remedied,' said Harker. 'In fact, I made myself damned unpopular down in the Mad House about that. I should think I put my foot in every Whitehall warrior's door. I pointed out that even Temporary Acting Sub-Lieutenants R.N.V.R. ought to know something about the weapon that will win the war. Besides ...' the captain paused, hope kindling wanly in his eye, '.... we *could* run into trouble....'

'Amen,' said Dickinson. 'The day we run into a Nazi raider with a crew of secondary schoolboys, that will be the day I get off and walk.'

'The sooner we get our radar the better, then,' replied the captain with a grin, 'to show us the *Hipper* in time.'

'In time for what?' said Dickinson. 'We couldn't get clear if we picked her up a hundred miles away.'

'Well, if this damn fog blows away by the morning I'll be able to see how the old girl behaves.'

'Yes, sir,' said Dickinson, staring into his glass.

'I intend poking my long nose into everything that goes on aboard,' said Harker. 'That's mainly why I'm here. I want to see every phase of training—see how these suède-shoe sailors shape up.'

'Yes, sir,' said Dickinson. Back in his own cabin again, he sat down heavily and looked at his photographs and drank a lot more gin. But it didn't help. It never did. This hurt, this terrible hurt, would be with him for as long as he lived ... *as long as he lived* . . . pray God that time were short. Perhaps this firebrand, this gong-hunting young destroyer ace, will kill us all. Bring on the *Hipper*. Let it be over soon—somehow. He looked at Lance's picture and saw there all the young faces that had stared up at him so wretchedly from the heaving boat in the fog. He saw the face of the slim youth gaping across the water, and it was the face of the boy his bayonets had killed long ago and the eager features of the new captain of *Constant*, then it was the cold face of his own son. . . . A great surge of compassion swept through his heart, meeting there, head on, the black tide of his own personal longing for oblivion. All of it twisted together into a great, heavy ulcer of despair. He leaned back in his chair, taut and tense, staring upwards at the beads of perspiration from the deckhead. He was like a sick man, or an insomniac, stretching and twisting away from the hurtful centre of the wound as if to escape, crying mutely for some healing knife, some magic cure-all, which would cut it out of him once and for all and leave him warm and untroubled again in the womb of a life that was like this lonely ship lost in the baying fog. He thought, They say that wounds heal quicker at sea. Oh, God, let it heal mine!

CHAPTER FOUR

IN the wheelhouse, blue-mittened hands alert on the wheel, eyes fixed on the green mineral glow of the gyro repeater, Leading Seaman 'Jumper' Cross, the quartermaster, opened his big, misshapen mouth and, like a crooner before a microphone, sang softly into the voicepipe:

'See *the dockyard mateys' children*
Sittin' on the dockyard wall,
Just like their fathers, doing —— all.
When they grow older they'll be dockyard mateys, too,
Just like their fathers, —— all to do.'

The Gunner, Lieutenant Price, heard him as he passed the other end of the voicepipe on the bridge, pacing up and down for exercise.

'Who's that, then?' he barked in his coarse, harsh Cornish voice. 'Bing Crosby at the wheel?'

'Sorry, sir.'

'If you *must* sing, let's have *Maggie May*," said the officer. 'Only save it for the ship's concert.'

Cross grinned. Good old Jan Price. You could tell he'd been a matelot himself. He still talked like one, even with two thick rings on his arm. The quartermaster turned to the cadet who was manning the engine room telegraphs by his side.

'It's about time you had a go,' he said.

'All right, Jumper,' said Ordinary Seaman Moore, 'just show me again, will you?' He was playing for time. He had been on watch in the wheelhouse for half an hour. During that time he had managed to learn how to manipulate the big brass handles of the telegraphs. 'Easy,' admonished Jumper Cross. 'Just pull 'em down and back again. Just imagine you're a barmaid at the *Rose and Crown*.' But the youth trembled when he thought of gripping that heavy, kicking wheel. It wasn't at all like steering a car or a speedboat, as he had imagined. When you moved that wheel you set 5,000 tons of steel swinging, a huge moving monolith that would simply *go on* swinging if you did not brake down her momentum before her head reached the new course. But if you over-corrected, those great bows down there would swing away again as if with a weary 'Make up your mind', and *Constant* would go on see-sawing all over the North Sea....

'You know, if you're going to be an officer an' give wheel orders to blokes like me, it isn't going to be much use if you don't know how to take the wheel yourself, is it?'

'No,' said Moore. 'Okay, I'll have a go now.'

'Good lad,' said Jumper. He cleared his throat and spoke into the voicepipe again. 'Wheelhouse-bridge.'

'Bridge,' rasped Price's voice.

'Permission for cadet rating to take the wheel, sir?'

'Permission granted.'

'Okay, mate,' said Jumper. 'Course o'-one-three, two-one-o' revs. She's all yours.' He slid aside and Moore nervously gripped the smooth spikes.

At once he felt the pull of the cruiser's weight against his slight muscles.

'Make your report, then,' said Jumper.

'Cadet rating Moore on the wheel, sir.'

'Very good.'

'Course o'-one-three, two-one-o' revs.'

'Very good.'

The boy looked at the needle representing the ship's head on the gyro repeater at eye level in front of him ... 014 ... The needle was swinging ... 015....

'Get back on your course, quartermaster!' The Cornish voice rasped out of the trumpet at his ear.

'Yes, sir,' said Moore, his heart beating heavily. 'What do I do, Jumper?'

'Don't panic, bash,' said Jumper. 'They'll put it on your slop chit if you put us on the rocks. Give her a slice of opposite rudder—not too much. Come on, chop-chop!'

'*Quartermaster!* I said *get back on your course!*' blared the brass mouth, 'and I don't mean Newton Abbot race-course neither!'

'Yes, sir, I'm sorry, sir,' said Moore, heaving the wheel to port as a disgusted snort blew down the voicepipe like a raspberry. The needle began to swing back ... 017 ... 016 ... 015 ... 014 ... he sighed his relief into the voicepipe ... 013 ... 012. ...

'Christ! Jumper. ...'

'You left it on too long,' said the leading hand patiently. 'You got to remember to put on opposite rudder just as she's reaching her course or she'll swing on way past it. Always anticipate the swing and correct before it's too late. Once she takes charge you've had it. And never put on too much—that's the secret of this lark, to keep the ship on course with as little movement of the wheel as possible ... *delicate*. ... Got it?'

'Yes, I think so,' said Moore.

'You're not steering your posh sports car now, you know.'

'Bridge-wheelhouse!' It was the Gunner again.

'Wheelhouse-bridge,' said Moore. His heart started pounding again.

'Starboard ten!'

'Starboard ten, sir!' He started to move the wheel. It felt as if the whole weight of green water from Scotland to Germany were shoving against his frail arms.

'Not too much, now,' said Jumper. 'Go on—make your report then. Chop-chop!'

'Um, ten of starboard wheel on, sir,' said Moore diffidently.

'Make your report in a seamanlike manner, quartermaster!' rasped the voice. 'If I had wanted "Um" I should have ordered "Um". Repeat!'

'Ten of starboard wheel on, sir!'

'That's better,' said the Gunner. 'Midships!'

'Midships, sir.'

'Go on, then, go on,' whispered Jumper hoarsely. 'Port your helm!'

Sweating, Moore pulled at the wheel, taking the swing off the ship so that she would steady on her new course.

'Wheel's amidships, sir.'

'Very good . . . Steady.'

'Steady, sir. . . .'

'Steer o'-two-two degrees.'

'Steer o'-two-two degrees, sir. . . .'

They tortured the poet for another twenty minutes, trying to make a helmsman out of him. Then he was relieved by another trembling beginner.

'Permission to change over, sir?' said Moore.

'Pemission granted. When you have done so, report to the bridge.'

'Aye, aye, sir.' He still felt silly when he said that, like a character out of *Treasure Island*. It was like 'Shiver me timbers!' or 'Heave-o, me hearties!'

On his way out of the wheelhouse he saw Wilsher.

'W . . . what's it like?' stammered the anxious lad.

'It's . . . it's like steering a planet through space,' said Moore.

The captain was on the compass platform.

'Come here,' he said, when Moore stumbled up the iron ladder to the bridge. 'What did you do in peacetime, Moore?'

'Er, I was at Cambridge, sir.'

'Oh, indeed. What were you reading?'

'Um, English, sir.'

'Um—English. I see. Then you must have come across some lines written by a gentleman anxious to "go down to the seas again" . . . How does it go? . . . "And all I ask is a tall ship and a star to steer her by". Well, Moore, after your recent experience do you think that a remark like that is pretty average cock?'

'Yes, sir,' said the poet, with a nervous grin.

'It's bloody awful poetry too, in my opinion,' said the captain. 'About as good as your helmsmanship. If you're going to be an officer and con a ship you must know exactly what your orders mean to the men who have to carry them out. All right, that'll do.'

Moore scuttled off the bridge, glad to escape. Jan Price, the Gunner, watched the boy go with a look of disgust on his weathered face. They're all the same, he thought, these modern kids. They let you down, they've got no guts at all. A man can't trust them or pass on to them what he's struggled all his life to learn. He was thinking again of his own son, for whom he had had such plans, such gruff, shy hopes, such burning ambitions, the son who had let him down, and his mother and the Service and his country.

The Gunner of *Constant* was a man for whom life was a ladder. By character, relentless effort and determination, Jan, the son of a Cornish fisherman drowned long ago at sea, had achieved the almost impossible. From boy enty as an orphan to a training ship he had risen, rung by rung, through the Lower Deck of the Royal Navy to officer's rank. He was a full lieutenant, a gunnery specialist and a seaman from whom very few answers concerning the sea were hidden.

But now he knew he could climb no farther up the ladder. His half ring perhaps, if he were lucky, and then retirement. The higher rungs where the air was rarefied and perfumed, these were out of his reach. He had strained resolution, brains and mental effort as far as they would go. Like any self-made man he resented the ugly fact that he had his limitations. There had been no time in his hard life to sow against the bitter times of want, when there was no longer anything hard and real to strive for. When that time came a simple man like the Gunner, locked within the very mortal world of phenomena, of concrete things and material conquests, would simply cease to be, his gnarled, muscle-bound soul petrified utterly by the first chill wind that howled in from the hell of eternal nothingness, where only the philosophic could live.

The Gunner felt this encroaching paralysis frighteningly, growing every day closer and more terrible like a stealthy tide. He could not keep it back, this awful lapse of being, for he had none of the mental weapons necessary to fight it, the large awareness of things having been drowned long ago, thrust under by the conquering need to be and do and make a mark on the flowing universe. Now he sensed, in all his misery, that all his achievements, all the things his striving, aching flesh had done, were about to be swept away in that great flood which swept away every conquest in the life of a man.

But if a man should drown, perhaps he could pass his little

glory on, flesh giving life to flesh which no spirit could refresh or keep alive, a man giving the pure gold of his dreams to his sons?

Jan Price had a son, an only son, and this son had been his swimmer in the dark, his torch bearer. For his son he had killed, not once but many times, the fatted calf. For his son he had fought and saved and planned. When his mother died young Price was already at Dartmouth, for it was Jan's prayer that his son should one day climb those far-off rungs which were out of his own reach, so that life would climb higher with the hands of the son, stepping on the shoulders of the father, the hewer of wood and the drawer of water who feared that his life might falter and drown in the dark.

But it was the son who faltered. In the year when war came again and threw mankind once more into the dark, flowing stream of time to sink or swim, when the old men, the veterans, went upon that sea, fighting to bring man's ship to anchor, young Price was dismissed from Dartmouth in deep disgrace. He had been found guilty of stealing money from other cadets —money he had spent on the wretched little local girl he had got into trouble. He came home and his father refused to see him, for he had let him down and an old man would die alone in the dark after all.

Could he trust the hands of a boy like that on the wheel of a ship, of a country's effort, of a fight to save mankind? They would all drown in the dark alone, for their sons were not strong enough to keep the ship on course.

With this bitterness in his heart, the Gunner was sent to an old training cruiser, whose ancient guns and fire control system were an insult to a good gunner, to be next to a hundred weak and wanting youths, to see them fail and falter at the hard tasks of survival, to see in them all the face of the son who had failed him when he faltered and fell down from the ladder ... Jan had an old man's bitterness now and despaired of the value and meaning of life.

Moore's class was in its first week, the seven days of trial and error in which they had to do all the things that seamen did—

keeping watch at lookout or on the guns, taking the wheel, manning a boat, rigging a boom in harbour, manning the side as quartermaster or side-boy, scrubbing the decks in bare feet—all the jobs, skilled or unskilled, difficult or monotonous, that fall to the lot of Jack-my-Hearty, the common matelot.

Through all this strange, bizarre and baffling nightmare, Jumper Cross, who was the leading hand in charge of their mess, led them with a firm but gentle hand. On the mess-deck, at stand-easy or in the dog watches in harbour they used to get him talking about the old Navy. There was white salt from a score of foreign commissions in his voice as he croaked.

He used to sit, big, brown, scarred, tarry hands round his chipped special kye mug with JUMPER L/S painted round the outside, his heavy jaw grim and set, brown sailor's eyes focused far away with a watchkeeper's deep-sea glance, and tell them about the tiddley ships he had served in, the great men he had known.

Someone or other was always asking him about The Gut in Malta, or The Sphinx in Algiers or Sister Street in Alexandria. But there were some things Jumper would not talk about—not in front of their tender ears. He became Grandpa Jumper then, and all he said was:

'Now never you mind about them places, you don't want to have nothing to do with them places. You just put your minds to things that really matter so that you can be somebody, not a ignorant bastard like me. If I ever catches you down Sister Street, officers or no officers, I'll use your guts for a necktie. There's things I seen down there Dad never did with Mum.'

'You must have seen a lot, Jumper,' said Moore, drawing him out cautiously. The poet loved to hear the matelot talk.

'Mate,' said Jumper weightily, 'plenty of blokes have seen a *lot*, but I've seen *everything*. I met an old chap once who'd served his time when the *Andrew* was still under sail, and I asked him what he felt—you know, looking back, like. He didn't answer me straight out but he coughed and rumbled a bit and his old eyes filled with tears and he suddenly cried out: "All the bastards are dead! All the bastards are dead!" That's the way I feel sometimes.'

They were squatting on the warm deck near the for'ard funnel, the sea boat's crew, all in black, shiny oilskins, the chinstays of their caps down against the bitter wind. But they were reasonably well sheltered from the wind here in the lee formed by the quivering hot flank of the funnel and the loom of the break of the fo'c'sle, with the dark pagoda of the bridge structure piled up upon the great shelf above them.

'Where were you before you joined the *Constant*, Hookey?' asked someone.

'Out in the Medi,' said the old sailor. 'Bit different to this bunch of bastards.'

'What's it like out there?' asked another boyish voice, eager and warm with shame, as if he were asking for a look at a dirty postcard.

'Flipping lush, mate,' said Jumper, 'only you got to go careful with the women; dead rotten most of 'em. I had an Arab bint in Algiers once. Zorah, her name was. She had her teeth all filed down to points. Number thirteen, the Rue Bologhin. . . . She was a lovely kid. I picked up a dose from her, though. You got to be careful. The whole Medi's like a woman, temperamental, blow hot blow cold but mostly hot, a dirty big black-haired slut lying naked in the sun, the cause of more trouble, more bloody ruin and murder than any woman ever born of human. The ships there must be, down the bottom there! I've seen some of 'em, when I was a diver, and all those poor sods that went down with 'em . . . I lost a good few mates out there. . . .' His coarse voice trailed away like a wisp of funnel smoke into the night.

Moore closed his eyes and thought of Italy and Greece and of himself back at school, lying in the long grass on a summer's day, listening to the gramophone playing the *Prélude à l'Après-midi d'un Faune* and dreaming sensuously of girls and love and a dream of Greece and the nakedness of a warm land under the sun, and then being a trembling faun in the back seat of a cinema with Jean or Pam or that dirty usherette who used to lean over you in the darkness if there was nobody about and let you . . .

'. . . Yeah,' Jumper was saying, 'the Medi's like a tart, she'll give you a good time and then a dose of the pox to remember her by. The Medi taught me how to live, how to enjoy life. Before the war, oh it was lush then—white awnings in the sun, brasswork gleaming, long make-and-mends when you just loafed and soaked up the sunshine.... It was all sunshine then.... Not like *this*....' He waved his mittened hand at the hooded, clouded night and the black, cold sea that stretched out towards the horizon of a war.

'You're a poet, Jumper,' said Moore.

'No, I leave that to you and Ella Wheeler Wilcox,' said the killick. 'I'd rather be in there doing things, not hanging about round the outside holding everybody else's coat and getting a second-hand thrill. You've got to get in there, you got to be *involved*, like ... that's what the *Andrew* teaches you.'

'And if you get a dose afterwards?' said Moore slyly.

'Oh well,' said Jumper, 'nothing venture nothing gain. Never win nothing if you don't put down your money. Just rotten luck and serve you right, you shouldn't have joined if you can't take a joke, that's all. Never be afraid to have a go, or you'll wake up when you're too old and wonder what you missed. Like us in peacetime, we had it real good out there in the sunshine and then, when the war came and we had to pay for it, I reckon there's none of those blokes sleeping down there under a thousand fathoms who wouldn't say "It was worth it", because they'd *lived*—see?' He lifted his head and sniffed the air. 'Cor, I thought I could smell the goats on Malta. I wouldn't mind being down The Gut now, in the Lucky Wheel or the Egyptian Queen. But them old whores have seen better days. Malta smells all right. It stinks of death like Pompey did after the big raids ... the *stink* of death everywhere. They're all bloody punchy, the Malts, keep trying to get up on their feet and then over comes Jerry and knocks 'em flat again. Little narrow streets, like gorges, all choked up with rubble, and a few clapped-out bars and cabarets and dance halls. And them wrecks in the harbour. I don't like to see them wrecks. There's the *Maori* there, with top of her foremast sticking out above Grand Harbour and there's another destroyer lying over against the jetty under Floriana with the whole of her bows amputated, like.... I don't like them wrecks, they make me bloody angry and miserable.

They were lovely ships once, fighting ships with good men in them ... all because the politicians sent them out to tackle Hitler's bloody blitzkrieg with no bleeding air cover. For years that bloody bastard waved a gun right under our noses. The politicians said they could talk him out of it and the pacifists pretended he wasn't there at all....

'And when he finally pulls the trigger, who gets hurt? Poor old Jack-my-Hearty—with no umbrella to keep the rain off. Politicians? I've spit 'em! My old man, sixty-one bleeding years old and flogging up and down the bleeding contraband blockade in a clapped-out armed merchant bastard cruiser when he should have been at home in front of the fire reading *Titbits*.... Took on the bleeding *Scharnhorst*, they did—and that was the end of my old man. And the pacifists and pansies and black marketeers all crawled into their little funkholes in the sand.... Not in Malta they didn't, though, they were all in it there, they had no choice. You get hit and you hit back, and God help you if you haven't got a gun, because all your pansy scruples and pangs of conscience won't help you then. That's all there is to it. That's war.'

They could sense his black mood as he squatted there, hunched in his funereal oilskin. *Constant* steamed on, the warm flank of the funnel shuddering in its stays behind them. It grew colder and more sullen about them. The sea was dark and angry. The ship rolled and seemed to shoulder it aside. Sometimes the moon came up through a threadbare patch in the dirty blanket of the sky and sent a cold needle of light through the darkness. The glitter would last a second or two, then flicker along the greasy mirror of the waves like a startled fish and die. All around them the sea rustled like a woman undressing.

Moore lay staring up into the night. It was all cold and strange and the future lay heavy on his mind. Once he fell into an uneasy doze but woke up shivering. Some of the men had lit cigarettes. They glowed like little camp fires in the darkness.

Then he got up and strolled about the humming, vibrating ship. He went over to the rail and stared down at the oily, supple sea. He spoke to one or two of the men on watch at the guns. He scrounged a cup of hot cocoa from the galley and sprawled on the warm deck among some of the ship's company, sipping his kye and listening to stories of foreign drafts and crafty trips up the line, wisps of chatter about lush bints and all-nights-in, of Sister Street Alex and The Gut in Malta and other places he'd never heard of. He loved the Navy then.

He thought of other things he loved about the *Andrew*. He thought of his short stay in Devonport Barracks—'Guz' as the matelots called it—where the barrack roads all sloped down to the glittering sea, where a fresh wind always blew in over Drake's Island and the Hoe, a salt breeze with the snap of canvas in it and the gusty freedom of the wide oceans where the Navy had kept station through centuries of grey weather, where there were always lovely bangers and chips and bread and butter in the canteen or a big, juicy pasty, a 'tiddie oggie' fat with meat and onion and potatoes, where there were runs ashore for a beer at the Long Bar or perhaps a passionate evening with that little slut from the Pay Office ... 'A cigaratte please, Jack,' she used to say afterwards.

He thought of the real joy of being a matelot, of wearing a tiddley suit with forty-inch bellbottoms and a tight jumper with zips down the side—and you still needed two men to get you out of it—of the matelot slang, which was a formal dance, with ritual question and answer:

'What ship, mate?'

'Destroyer.'

'Destroyers—I've spit 'em!'

'Well spit us a couple more then, we need 'em!'

He thought of the thrill and freedom of a run ashore with pound notes in the pocket, the excitement mixed with foreboding of a new ship....

He loved the Navy. It was no good trying to hide it. He was all for it, as Jumper would say. That was another matelot phrase he had learned, like 'Never volunteer for anything.'

But as he thought all these things, it grew colder. The cruiser steamed on through the night. She seemed invulnerable, a symbol in steel of irresistible power and strength thrusting and shouldering the sea aside. Then, now and again, the sea would suddenly punch her thin, bare flanks, and the whole great structure would jump and shudder, suddenly turned to a jelly of mad atoms. The rivets jarred and danced in their holes, the skin of metal trembled as if under the whip, a ripple ran through the shell from stem to stern.

Every time this happened his heart seemed to give a lurch as his brittle surroundings shook mightily, then settled once more inside the formalised shipshape that was the cruiser, back into an uneasy armistice with the sullen, ever-resentful sea.

'Is this my world,' he thought, 'the sailor's world?'

It could never be a home, this ship of war. She had been built entirely round her power to destroy. Her men came a poor second, living precariously wherever there happened to be a small space between the machinery, in ill-lit vibrating cubby-holes. At sea they ate here, snatching quick badly cooked meals, and slept here, in a stuffy nest of swinging hammocks, breathing foul air, in between weary hours of red-eyed wakefulness at the guns, on the bridge, down in the boiler rooms or bolted inside little cells on watch. 'Iron slums', a politician had called these ships.

It was even worse on draft. Then you were just tramps in navy blue, lost on the quaking wasteland between one ship and the next, with that cold, panicky feeling you got when you were in the draft lorry with your bag and hammock, watching the barrack gates of Pompey, Chatham or Guz slip away, and wondering what you were in for....

You were an exile then, your home a hammock, at the mercy of mysterious, Kafka-like drafting offices with little, cobwebbed windows uncleaned since Jutland, that snapped open long after you had given up all hope of their ever opening, glared and smelled badly of sweat and tea fumes and shouted for station-cards and pay-books, then slammed shut on quaking freedom like workhouses. At sea you had at least a kind of home, a floating outpost tied by the mother string to Chatham or Pompey or Devonport, wherever the parent workhouse stood. On draft you were all dispossessed. The last ship might have been a small hell: the next might be a kind of heaven. In between, you were lost in the limbo of the draft.

Moore lay and worried, trying to doze. He watched the masthead, miles up aloft, as it rolled from star to star. He watched one star as it did a formal dance with the truck of the mast, like someone trying to fix a silver doll to the top of a swaying Christmas tree with its roots in water instead of solid earth. *And a star to steer her by....*

He stared at the star, wondering how far away it was from the earth, from the North Sea, from the voyaging ship. It would be light years distant, all the beautiful abstractions and equations of quanta and fourth dimensions away, unreal, unimaginable, irrelevant to human striving, a mirage in the mind's eye, a lamia. What good would it do him if someone voyaged to the moon and the stars? What good were all beautiful things, music and poems and crystal thoughts like glass? People wrote symphonies, sonnets; painted pictures, made all man's little miracles —and thought they had experienced the only final, formal face of reality. Men marooned themselves in starry, swaying towers to look for reality or God or self. Airmen yearned to go in rockets to the planets; sailors searched endlessly for new Americas. To what end? What good did it do him and all those around him now, stirring and moaning in their troubled sleep, voyaging on towards the dark coastline of a war? Thought, art, which created music and poems and crystal science, created also the hunched, crouching bulk of the guns. It was all borne of the same mad megalomaniac dream that had begun all this....

What good does all the striving, all the planning and the dreaming do? he asked himself. In the end it is always the same—a sailor staring into the night, wondering who he is and where he is bound for, never sure of anything—ship, sea, self or destination, with every landfall a lie, every port a mirage.

What good is doing, acting—*things*? What is the real world? Surely not *this*, the mad carnival of the animals, the frantic self-preservation of the Ark against the Flood, a man alone, on perpetual watch, locked in a metal box ... a ghost ship in outer space between the stars, revolving eternally in free orbit, an outpost shimmering on a desert hill....

The star was still there and the masthead, unchanged, dancing together, and the deck warm and real as he touched it like feeling a woman's breast in the night. Now it seemed as if the star were moving, wandering the desolation of the sky, while he and the ship and all the men in her were fixed, not really moving at all, not really going anywhere at all, but fixed in the middle of this ancient sea, with stars burning and falling about them like birds of omen whose significant attitudes they could not interpret, and the sea rushing past them with lovely, lustful voices whose enigmas they would never unravel. . . . He began to doze, with all of it a sleepy poem in his head.

He woke again soon after. The scene had changed. Moonlight had broken through and now threw its silver bangles on the water. He went and looked down at the white, rushing foam of the ship's thrusting motion and felt the sway of her flanks against the sea. The sense of stillness and timelessness left him and the urgent, passionate present returned. The ship shouldered forward with a surge of longing into the night, and the sea itself was the stillness and the mystery, a wide, limitless world to be explored and conquered. He looked down at the dark water, wondering at the world beneath the waves.

CHAPTER FIVE

'HEAVE-O, heave-o, heave-o, lash up and stow!'

The marine's coarse shout swirled round the lumpy, gently swinging hammocks like a chill wind off the sea.

The cadets shivered and groaned. This was the moment they had all come to dread most of all, this awful baptism into the working day. Heavy-eyed and stale they hugged their sleep sullenly, stealing a few extra minutes from the urgent call of war.

'Heave-o, heave-o, heave-o, lash up and stow!' The bellow was loud in Moore's ear as the marine, bent double, squeezed under the nettles that supported the end of his hammock. He tensed himself and waited for the next inevitable step in the routine. As the marine passed under the swollen bulge where the cadet's body weighed the hammock down he heaved upwards, jerking the swaying canvas and the lumpy body inside it into the air. It happened every morning, without fail.

It would not have happened if Moore had been quicker to stake his claim to a good billet when they had first come aboard. When he did come to sling his hammock for the first time all he could find was a place right over the gangway which ran fore and aft down the inboard side of the mess tables. Every morning the sadist who called the hands rose up like a sporting dolphin as he crawled down the gangway and bounced Moore up towards the deckhead.

In a way he was grateful for the rude awakening. After the earthquake the snugness of the hammock was gone for good. You might as well turn out, then you might get to the wash-place in time to grab a basin and enjoy the luxury of a shave before breakfast. But you must get out before your body had time to sink back into the womb of the blanket. It was no good waiting for the second bump when the marine came back along the passage. It was too late then, and the washplace was full of snarling, scratching sailors and steam.

Moore raised his head from the frowsty blanket which he had rolled round him like a tube. The tube was open at both ends, leaving his feet sticking out bare and cold into the hammock nettles. He looked outboard over the edge of the taut canvas at his nearest neighbour. It had become his habit to watch the performance which Jack McCutchen put on every morning.

Mac had taken instantly to lower deck life. One matelot habit he had adopted was the involved and intricate ritual of the early morning fag. Moore watched fascinated as McCutchen yawned, broke wind loudly, then reached for the top of the square-sectioned steam-pipe above his head. Already laid out on the pipe was the white cylinder of the cigarette, put there the night before. Alongside it lay a matchbox. On the matchbox lay a match. It was rather like the twig that grew on the branch that grew on the tree that grew.... First the hand went with the unerring aim of two weeks' practice straight as an arrow to the cigarette, which it transferred with similar precision to McCutchen's open mouth, like a worm to the maw of a voracious fledgling. The hand returned like a crane for another load and came back with the match. This it transferred to the other hand and returned yet again for the matchbox. Then left hand crossed right, scratched up a flame and lit the tilted touch-hole of the gasper. Combustion effected, the smoker fired a two-gun salvo from his nostrils. The drifting smoke always crossed Moore's bows and made him cough. But he never failed to admire the performance, which had the perfection and precision of a Swiss watch or a well-trained gun's crew swinging into action, all the more so since the smoker did not once open his eyes during the entire performance.

McCutchen had picked up this habit from the matelots of *Constant*'s ship's company. He had learned to roll his cigarettes as well, from naval issue tobacco and paper. 'Ticklers' the matelots called these gaspers, although no would-be officer was expected to go in for them. But Jack McCutchen seemed to prefer the company of the lower deck. It looked sometimes to his classmates as if he would have preferred to have been an ordinary matelot in the ship's company himself. The snobs concluded that he was no gentleman and would therefore never make an officer: the others were amused by his rapidly swelling vocabulary of lower deck slang and his gradual assumption of a matelot's habits. It seemed that, in spite of all his burning ambition to soar aloft, Jack McCutchen, who had funked the mast at *Ganges*, was an earthbound creature.

Moore sympathised with him because he himself loved the colour and queer fashions of the lower deck. In fact, he carried a little red-covered notebook about with him in which he recorded the lurid phrases which fell from the lips of *Constant*'s ship's company. 'Bullshit beats brains' was the very first laconic entry. An elderly stripey had passed that piece of doubtful advice on to him during his first day on board. Jumper's word was always worth hanging on. 'Cor chase my winger round the wash-house!' he said once. But the gem of Moore's collection so far had sprung all hot from the agitated lips of the assistant divisional officer, an affected gentleman of the R.N.V.R. with a beautiful beard, who had angrily told a disgusted seaman petty officer, 'It doesn't matter a fish's tit which way the damn thing goes!' apropos of making fast a boat's falls.

But the songs, the lower deck songs, were the real treasures of Moore's little anthology. In it was to be found the sad lament of *Maggie May*, who:

Betrayed all the sailors
And the captains of the whalers
The first time that they put in from sea,

that lady of Lime Street who was so well loved, even when she had pawned all her matelot victim's clothes, that he could lament,

Oh my darlin' Maggie May
They 'ave taken you a-wayee . . .
And I'll never see my darlin' any more. . . .

Maggie May's gentlemen friends, like most matelots ashore,

were always 'seen off'. None of them ever got 'up homers' with his 'feet under the table'. He might, if he were lucky, 'fill his boots' for one glorious 'all night in' with the lady, but in the cold light of dawn his was the sad story of:

Nabob, son of Paybob,
Who didst journey forth to Gosport
In search of an all night in,
And on his way he fell among thieves. . . .

All this the poet put into his little book. For one who loved words and coloured phrases this argot was pure delight.

On lookout duty one middle watch he found himself thinking of Devonport and Plymouth and what a matelot did when he went ashore. He thought of the eggs and chips and the visit to the boozer, of the sad, sordid women whom the simple sailor went with, and he began to make up a ballad. . . .

Sailor, sailor, handsome Jack,
I'll have a gin and knock it back,
Treat me rough like sailors do,
I'm a tramp the same as you.

It sounded like a number from the matelot review, a folksy ballad for sailors to sing to a small guitar. He was trying to decide how the last verse should go when he heard with a shock an angry voice shouting at him. He turned quickly round and saw the Gunner's furious face. Writing a sailor's ballad and being a sailor were two different things. He abandoned the sad harlot in the clover and became a bad sailor in trouble.

Old Jan gave him a man-sized dressing-down for failing to report a light fine off *Constant*'s starboard bow, and the poet withdrew sulkily, whipped by the actual world once more into the hollow shell of his thoughts. Ten minutes later he tried to redeem himself by reporting another light. When this 'light' turned out to be a star low on the horizon the Gunner was very angry and his wrath lashed the young man raw, so that he began to despise himself bitterly for a starstruck fool who could never recognise 'On or in front of the foremast, or if a vessel without a foremast, then in the forepart of the vessel, a bright white light, so constructed as to show an unbroken light over an arc of the horizon of twenty points of the compass' or a real ship on a real sea for what it was—no symbol for poets to trick out in the fairy lights of images, but a voyaging, doing thing with an objective in the ordinary life of man, a dangerous thing which could come out of the night on a collision course and sink all his golden dreams and all the humble yearnings of the men in the ship.

All this the Gunner who, this watch, held the ship and her men in his tough, sure old hands knew by instinct. All this the young future officers, the new leaders, must learn. The Gunner, in his personal disillusionment and bitterness, despaired of their ever learning it. Moore, the dreamer, felt dimly but desperately that he must learn it, or go under completely himself, both as writer and man, as sailor and singer. He tried to kick overboard Jack-my-Hearty, with his animal ambitions of boozers that never closed and endless all nights in with lush tarts, the little hand-to-mouth world of the perpetual underdog. He tried to drown the poet too, with his sad, sour little ballads, forever trying to build a life from the straw of other men's loves and sorrows. He thought of the ship in the night, voyaging towards a war, and of the men who had designed and created her speed and beauty and usefulness, the men who navigated her on behalf of all their fellow men, of the men who never slept, who built and created and schemed, even in their dreams, and did not spend their hours on watch seeing the stars on the far, unknown, unreal horizon.... He forgot his ballad and instead recited fiercely to himself.

'Both in safety and in doubt
Always keep a good lookout;
In danger with no room to turn,
Ease her—stop her—go astern.'

I *will* get through, I *will* succeed, this *is* my world! he told himself desperately.

Each morning he awoke and forced himself to grip that steam-pipe casing over his head, from which his hammock swung, push aside his copy of Dylan Thomas's poems, heave himself up and lower himself in his singlet and pants—a matelot's night attire—to the cold steel deck. Struggling into his bell-bottoms he would grab his washing gear and make his way through the maze of humming, vibrating passageways to the tiny iron cell in the bowels of the ship which was the seamen's washplace.

There were eight bowls, thick with scum and dirt, in this little place, for a hundred men and more, and it was a case of every man for himself each morning. You had to be dead lucky, and up very early, to get a wash and shave. And if an officer cadet should dare to appear for instruction with a day's growth, even of adolescent fluff . . .

Moore was the first in the washplace this morning. He shaved in agony with a rusty blade he picked up in one of the filthy basins, cutting himself in a dozen places. By and by, during the afternoon watch in the classroom, his face began to itch and burn. It was so painful by the end of the afternoon that he reported sick.

The sick bay attendant took one look at the angry rash and said, 'Impetigo, mate.' They painted the poet's jaw and neck with a dark blue salve called gentian violet. It was about the colour of ancient woad and marked him out like a leper from all the others. He went round bearing the reward of his carelessness like a shameful brand. He became the butt of a thousand jokes and shafts of matelot and R.N. wit. The captain noticed him with a shout of delight and called him 'the painted savage'.

It had become known that he was a writer and now he went about as if publicly branded with it by the blue paint, enduring the jibes of the sailors. Moore was no martyr. Just at this time he repudiated his scribbling, hating it and ashamed of it with all his heart, fiercely longing to be accepted as a sailor, as one of them.

But it seemed that whenever he tried to wield the blade of the man in action he tripped over it and fell flat on his face. A place in the sun of active life seemed to be denied to him; only the moonlight of the contemplative life was meant to be his, it seemed. It had always been like that, always grabbing at the ripeness and over-reaching, falling flat on his face. And yet, of all people, he knew so well the beauty and fullness of real things—things never meant to be his to have and to hold, always out of reach. And what did he have to show for it, this lofty role of observer? Just a few miserable, scribbled verses and one or two little stories. He was neither sailor nor artist. He was a failure.

In his wretchedness he became drawn to other unhappy souls. Wilsher was another young man in limbo, lost between the nothingness of adolescence and the achievements of manhood. Wilsher's handicap was a cruel one, a physical deformity, a scar. He stuttered. He stuttered so badly that it was hard to believe that he had come into the Navy from the stage.

'How on earth did you get on—speaking your lines, I mean?' he was often asked.

'I . . . somehow it was all right, I never did it then,' said the miserable young man. 'One could forget oneself, you know—lose oneself in the part.'

'Being an officer's playing a part, mate,' McCutchen would say, in his case a sufferer from that cancerous fear of things which were too high for him, but ever ready nowadays with the bromides of the lower deck. 'Bullshit beats brains, you know!'

'But this is *real*!' said Wilsher. In his sincerity and absolute certainty, he forgot to stammer. 'This isn't acting, this is real, it involves you, the real you . . . it *matters*!' He became aware that he was speaking clearly and forcefully. It was different when he was on lookout wanting to report a light, or a telephone number at his post on the bridge or at the gun with the vital job of relaying range and bearing to the layer and trainer. . . .

'What would you do, Wilsher,' Dickinson had said to him sternly, 'if you were officer of the watch and could not deliver an urgent wheel order which meant the difference between dodging a Stuka's bomb and losing the ship?'

'I . . . I . . .' the boy agonised, like a deaf mute straining to speak.

But the other two cadets understood him now. They were three young men with a young man's bitter problem, plunged neck and crop into a harsh world where war intensified the jungle rules of life, heightened its dangers and tensions and the urgent need to act. They all feared this life and all felt obscurely that it could be their salvation. It was a battle for them, each to overcome his private shame, a struggle for the self, a desperate need to succeed and be real in a world of illusion.

They were all in limbo and the struggle seemed to be defeating them all. The ladder was too steep, the climb too frightful. Like *Constant*'s towering foremast that loomed so high, at once surface and symbol, the task was too tall for them. McCutchen feared he could never climb it, and Moore feared to lose himself among the stars at its aery top, while Wilsher's nightmare was to be doomed forever to be lookout there, voiceless and tongueless, with the great monster bows of war and life looming ever closer, the terrible eyes of her hawse holes in baleful glare upon him....

For them, this taking to the sea was like being launched into life itself. A rough sea was a jungle, or a calm, sunlit ocean, unbelievable balm to the buffeted spirit. But in no sense was the sea a friend, always only an enemy to be fought and tamed. Moore, being a sort of pseudo-intellectual, thought of what Freud had said about the sea being symbolic of the womb. Being also a sort of pseudo-sailor he was able to think as well of the sea as the sea, and to live with it and on it as such, however badly. Womb or sea, symbol or surface, whichever word you happened to like, the sea was either a salty slough that drowned you or a green sunlit fire from which you arose refreshed and as a man.

The ship dominated them completely. They fumbled and stumbled their way through the curriculum laid down for them, but they knew all the time that they were play-acting, pretending to be sailors. None of it was real. Because of this many of them could not give of their best, for they could not believe in what they were doing. The ship steamed out and steamed in again, went slowly up and down past the purple hills, round May Island and up as far as the Inchcape Rock, but in no sense were they a part of her or of anything real. She might as well have been a pleasure steamer. Her classroom could just as easily have been ashore, and the brief spells of watch-keeping they did were so scrappy as to be almost valueless. As a mere testing ground for character, *Constant* was an expensive luxury, for the shortness of the spell which each cadet had aboard her and the utter alien strangeness of the whole experience were not calculated to bring out his manly virtues. It was not enough to state baldly that a boy had survived the *Constant* without going to pieces. This said very little for him. When he left her he was still a raw civilian masquerading in navy blue.

All this the new captain had been sent to find out, and he spared no pains to do so. He interviewed personally and intensively every officer and man of the ship's company and especially the instructors: he spoke with many of the cadets to try and assess their reactions. He pried and probed and questioned and made copious notes. He was everywhere.

One result was a tightening up in discipline. The very appointment of Harker told the instructors plainly that *Constant* had been found wanting. If the Admiralty thought the future officers she produced were not good enough, then they must have a poor opinion of the men who taught them.

Anything frivolous or inefficient was from this time on ruthlessly stamped out. When Wilsher, best in his division at signals, got both eyes full of smuts from the funnel at a flashing exercise and could not read the stuttering lamp in the flagdeck, his own stuttered explanation sounded lame and was brushed aside by Dickinson, who thought he was shirking. Wilsher offered almost tearfully to take another Morse test to prove himself, but he was told sharply 'not to waste the Navy's time!'

'You will have worse then smuts in your eyes in battle,' said Dickinson roughly. 'Gunsmoke and cordite fumes and God knows what else—and you will *have* to read signals then!'

Poor Wilsher got noticeably more bloody-minded after that and his stammer increased to such a degree that when the captain gave him a wheel order to pass down to the helmsman the words stuck in his throat so long that he had to be sent off the bridge.

'It just won't do. An officer must be able to make himself clearly and instantly understood,' said the captain.

Moore was next on the bridge for instruction on this occasion.

'How is the Ancient Briton this morning?' asked Harker. 'Take a bearing of that ship!' He flung out his hand, pointing to starboard. Moore bent his blue-painted chin to the azimuth mirror. 'Alter course to o'-three-five! Come on, jump to it!'

Caught between the two orders, Moore hesitated, and was damned.

'What with poets, actors who don't know their lines and all the other Orientals, I am beginning to wonder whether this is a ship of His Majesty's Navy or tea-time at the British Council,' said Harker. 'Moore, the bridge of a ship of war is no place to play *Hamlet*.'

'This isn't exactly a ship of war, sir,' gulped Moore sulkily, his heart beating fast at his daring.

The captain, instead of blowing up in a cloud of steam, as everyone on the bridge fully anticipated, stared at him quizzically for a moment. 'Moore,' he said at last, 'if I may quote one poet to another, "You speak better than you know and beyond your understanding." Now take that awful blue face off my bridge.'

The poet shambled away down the ladder. That night after supper they gathered as usual in the mess to peel the potatoes for the next day's dinner. Wilsher took a vicious swipe at a large spud and sliced it in half. 'I w . . . wish that was Captain b . . . bloody Harker!' he said.

'Now then,' said Jumper, 'watch your language, mate.'

'I wish the b . . . bastard was in hell!' said the miserable young man.

'Officers go to heaven, mate,' said Jumper, 'with all the bleedin' parsons. Only matelots go to hell. Didn't I never tell you about the two old stripeys who met me down in hell?'

'No, Jumper, go on!'

'All right, then. Well, one day two three-badge A.B.s found themselves warming their fannies down by the big fire. " 'Ello, wings," says one, "fancy seeing you 'ere. I thought you went to the other place." "Well, I did," he said, "but I got kicked out." " 'Ow did that 'appen?" said the other bloke. "Well, it's a long story, mate," said the first matelot, "but I'll tell yer.

'"I reports with me bag and 'ammock at the Pearly Gates. I knocks. Out of a window up aloft a bloke sticks his head out. ''Op it!' he said, 'we're full up.' 'Draft chit,' I says. 'Oh,' he says, 'you better come in then, but you'll 'ave to kip down in the cherubims' 'eads for tonight.'

'"In the morning I falls in on the parade, in the back row, on the right. Out comes the Chief Buffer Angel, big pair of wings, dirty big 'alo round 'is 'ead, and says, 'Right. Those on the left—Creator's quarters sweepers. Away you go and get your brooms on the double! Those in the middle—Pearly Gate painting party. Away you go laughing! Those on the right—'arping party!'

'"They gives me a 'arp and I 'arps—all the forenoon and half the afternoon as well. Misses me tot and me dinner. I'm proper chokka, me. Next morning I says to myself 'Mate,' I says, 'this time you got to be smart.' I falls in in the *middle*.

'"Out comes the Chief Buffer Angel, dirty big 'alo, big pair of wings. 'Right,' he says. 'Those on the left Creator's quarters sweepers. Away you go on the double! Those on the right—Pearly Gate painting party. Away you go laughing! Those in the middle—'arping party!'

'"I get me 'arp and I 'arps—all the forenoon, all the afternoon and both the dogs. Misses me tot, me dinner and me tea. I'm chokka to the eyebrows. Next morning I says, 'This time, mate, you got to box clever.' I falls in on the *left*.

'"Out he comes. 'Right,' he says. 'Those on the right—Creator's quarters sweepers. Away you go! Those in the middle—Pearly Gate painting party. Away you go laughing!' I've 'ad enough. I steps out.

'"Buffs," I says, "I do not —— 'arp!"

'" 'You wot?' he says.

'"I do not —— 'arp,' I says.

'" 'Right,' he says. 'Get yer 'alo!'

'"Then he marches me off to see the Old Man.

'"' 'Alt!' he says. 'Off 'aloes!'

'" 'Well, what's this 'ere man been a flippin' well doin' of?' says the Old Man.

' " ' 'E did,' says the Chief Buffer, 'use insultin' language to a Chief Petty Angel, to wit, "I do not —— 'arp!" '

' " 'Did you really say that?' says the Skipper, looking a bit shocked like.

' " 'Yes,' I says, 'an' I —— well meant it an' all!'

' " 'Right!' he says. 'Seven days Hell!'

' "That's 'ow I got down 'ere—an' you still can't get near the fire for Chief Stokers!" '

It did them good to laugh. 'Blimey,' said Jumper, 'anyone'd think you was peeling onions, not spuds!'

But their laughter was swiftly cut short when Dickinson appeared in the mess.

'Someone,' he said wryly, 'has deposited a load of filth in the motor cutter. I want two volunteers to clean it up and scrub the boat out at once.'

'All right, sir,' said Jumper, 'I'll see to it.'

When the Divisional Officer had gone he turned to them. 'All right you shower,' he said. 'Who was cooks?'

Moore and McCutchen looked at each other. 'We were,' they said together.

'Well, you want to look where you're chucking the gash next time,' said the leading hand. 'All right, let's get weaving.'

Out in the cold and dark they climbed over the guard-rails and inched their way fearfully along the swaying boom which stuck out from the ship's side and from which the ship's boats swung in the black stream below. Shivering with cold and trembling with apprehension they lowered themselves slowly to a sitting position on the boom, then, clinging desperately to its slippery surface, they scrambled awkwardly down the white ladder into the heaving boat.

The gash from supper which they had thrown carelessly over the side had fouled the well-scrubbed bottom boards and gleaming paintwork of the cutter. On hands and knees they began to scrape it off and wash the paintwork clean.

By ten o'clock, stiff with cold, they had just about finished the job. Jumper came on deck and shouted to them to come inboard.

To navigate ladder and boom was even harder now. It was

colder and they were wet and numb. As McCutchen climbed inboard he suddenly felt the boom shudder under him, heard a despairing cry from behind, and looked round just in time to see Moore's cap floating away in the direction of Rosyth.

When they hauled him out the poet could not speak. They rubbed him down, dosed him with some of Jumper's illegal bottled tot and tucked him up in his hammock. His cap Jumper took along to the galley, to put inside an oven to dry. It came out several sizes too small and served to make Moore even more of a pariah than ever.

It was a miserable night. To make matters worse they discovered that the Jacob's ladder on the boom had only just been painted, and each of them had a sticky white replica right down the front of their uniforms....

'Proper chokka, me,' said McCutchen. 'Chokka to the eyebrows.'

CHAPTER SIX

'THE rules concerning lights shall be complied with in all weathers from sunset to sunrise, and during such time no other lights which may be mistaken for the prescribed lights or impair their visibility may be exhibited.'

Painfully they were negotiating the International Regulations For Preventing Collisions At Sea.

'What would you do if you were to see the *K.G.V* flying three black balls at her yardarm?' asked Lieutenant Berryman. He pointed at Ordinary Seaman the Honourable Guy Stott.

'Er, I should rather tend to give her a wide berth,' said the Honourable.

'Why?'

'Well, I don't really know, actually....'

'What do the three black balls mean, then?'

'Um ... yellow fever?' suggested the youth diffidently.

Berryman, ex-chief petty officer, ex-warrant officer, sixty years old and a seaman since boy-entry on the *Conway*, stared at him.

'Christ,' he said flatly. 'Yellow fever.' He shook his head, sat down and poured himself a glass of water. 'Tell him what three black balls means, someone,' he said sadly.

'Sir,' said one of the bright boys, 'I am not under command, not making way through the water.'

'That's right,' said the old seaman, 'and I hope they carry plenty of spare ones in any ship you lot get drafted to.' He looked disgustedly at the Honourable Guy. 'You're as wet as a scrubber, Stott,' he said. 'and not half as useful. I don't know how you got this far.'

'No, sir.'

Berryman craned forward and peered at the aristocrat matelot suspiciously.

'Did you wash your neck this morning?'

'Yes, sir!'

'Are you sure?'

The Honourable blushed. 'Well, actually, I couldn't get near the wash-basins, sir.'

'Adrift again, I suppose?'

'Yes, sir.'

'By the way, what exac'ly were you doing wandering about the fo'c'sle yesterday afternoon? You looked like a spare wot-name at a wedding.'

It was a fair description of the gormless Guy.

'Well, actually I thought we were supposed to be doing something there,' he said. 'I wondered where all the other chaps were, as a matter of fact.'

'I see,' said Berryman. 'I was hoping you might fall over the side.'

There were among the cadets the bright, the misty and the thoroughly tarnished, and the Honourable Guy was without exception the most tarnished, the most obscure of mind, they had ever had aboard, so completely hidden was the shining silver of that intelligence which distinguishes man from the brutes. He wandered about the ship in a perpetual daydream, always adrift, ever unwashed and unshaven. If ever a unit of His Majesty's Navy could be said to be 'not under command, not making way through the water', it was Ordinary Seaman Stott. In his short career in the Royal Navy he had left behind him a long succession of shocked and startled faces, officers and petty officers unable to believe their ears. There was C.P.O. Sprout at *Ganges*, who had never been quite the same man since Stott had triumphantly identified a long splice as a plug of tobacco, in the seamanship exam.

By now he had made a definite impression upon the *Constant*. One bright morning on the fo'c'sle the division had fallen in for leaving harbour, when it was seen that Ordinary Seaman Stott was capless.

'What is that man doing without a cap?' shouted the captain from the bridge.

'Where is your cap, Stott?' asked Dickinson sternly.

'Well, sir,' said the Honourable brightly, 'it was such a wizard day, sir, I left it downstairs.'

The captain, when he was told, refused utterly to believe what he had heard. Even now, every time he saw the cadet he wanted to stretch out a hand and touch him to see if he was real. . . . He looked forward with pleasure to the day when Stott would have to come to the bridge for his captain's interview. Who could guess what priceless surrealisms might fall from his mouth then?

If the Seamanship Manual was literally a closed book to Stott, 'Torpedoes' was a fantastic enigma. He began with a vague idea that the subject had to do with the missiles that were fired by submarines. But the instructor spent all his time talking about electricity, juggling with mystic symbols called Voltage, Current, Resistance, Amperes and Ohms. 'Electricity,' said the instructor, 'may be defined as an energy which may be converted from one type of energy to another.'

'Just like us,' whispered Moore to Wilsher, who grinned sardonically. About the only thing Stott felt he could vaguely understand was the structure of the 'simple cell'—'carbon rod, carbon dust and manganese surrounded by an exciting paste . . .' as the instructor told them. Stott felt a sympathy, a family affinity with this harmless creature, whose energy, they were told, 'soon falls off and never properly recovers'. He especially liked the bit about 'exciting paste'. He felt is must be *jolly* exciting, like a new shade in interior decorating. Like Moore, the poet, he had made his mark on the *Constant*. It was a wonder she did not vomit them both up upon the waters, like twin Jonahs out of the belly of the whale.

As for gunnery, they felt very much after the heart of the subaltern back from Dunkirk who had complained about 'the *noise*! And the *people*!'

This was unfortunate, for all *Constant*'s senior officers were gunners by trade. Whale Island, the Navy's secretly beloved Alcatraz, had spawned them all, especially the captain and the Gunner, Jan Price, and moulded them inside the strait-jacket of 'gas and gaiters'. To them, guns were the all-important things, the whole reason for a warship's being. This conviction they were determined at all costs to pass on to their pupils.

Gunnery, therefore, came highest in importance in the syllabus. In a world of violence, especially in a service dedicated to its use in the protection of civilised man, the science of hurting the enemy was the sailor's sole reason for existence. The cadets were not allowed to forget this elementary fact of life.

The captain set about making them all gun-minded. Before his appointment to *Constant*, instruction had been confined to a few dummy runs and one practice shoot on the fo'c'sle six-inch. The great gun became a carousel of frightful motion and clangour, and dazed cadets were jerked through the complicated evolution of firing a six-inch shell in the general direction of Germany like bewildered puppets in the grip of a robot, as frightening a brute as a hunter or a fast sports car. The captain was a young man himself, but he loved hunters and fast cars almost as much as he loved a beautiful, tearaway destroyer with white water plunging down her vibrating flanks, and her guns and tubes hunched like poised beasts of prey. His was a fighter's creed and he saw in the eighty boys under his command eighty raw acolytes.

Logically enough, they started with the smallest weapon, the tommy-gun. '. . . The spring motivates forward movement, the explosion causes backward movement . . .' and worked their way upwards.

Jan Price stripped the Lewis gun of all its secrets for them. 'Gas generated by the explosion follows the bullets up the barrel and some enters the gas chamber *this* is of sufficient velocity to force back the piston and thus the *striker-pin* the *piston* is connected to the *spring* by cogs and the backward movement of the piston winds up the spring to its maximum tension of twelve to fourteen pounds the piston and striker pin are held in this position by the *seer* until the trigger is pressed. . . .' It was like the science lab at school on a drowsy summer day, with the shouts of the cricketers coming in through the windows, sharp and faraway as sea-birds in their holiday of air.

Old Jan knew his guns as only an ex-Whale Island gunnery instructor can. His harsh bark was like the voice of the gun itself which lay under his sure, practised hands as he demonstrated. 'Remove the magazine ... ease the barrel spring ... lubricate the top of the breach ... remove the shoulder piece, handgrips, trigger cover, plate and trigger-casing ... drain out any water in the gun body ... lubricate the trigger mechanism ... reassemble ... cock the gun ... ease the spring ... re-cock.' He lifted the heavy Vickers machine-gun and pointed it at Moore, as if he were tired of seeing that blue-daubed symbol of ignorant, indolent civilian youth.

The poet was fascinated by the cascade of hard metallic phrases which spurted from old Jan's gun muzzle of a mouth. He himself had memorised things like the superbly Gilbertian 'Lubricatelocklightlyandlockguidewayswithoutmovingthelockor-unloading'. Then one day Jan astounded them all by stripping and reassembling the lock of a Lewis gun with his eyes shut. It was an amazing *tour de force*, depressing some of them with its revelation of their own ignorance, encouraging others to harder efforts.

Jumper Cross demonstrated to them the Oerlikon quick-firing cannon.

'They said this gun was fit for scrap-iron,' he said, as they all crowded round him on the wing of the flag-deck. 'All the bleeding armchair admirals with brass all over their caps and no brains in their heads. If we'd had it sooner a lot more good lads'd be alive today. It was the thing we wanted to keep the Stukas off.'

He patted the long, black barrel. 'I was in the *Killarney*, one of Lord Louis' Fighting Fifth Flotilla, an' I knocked down three of the bastards with one of these.' He stared out to sea, where a squadron of torpedo-bombers from the new carrier *Invincible* was deploying to make a mock attack on *Constant*. It was the grey North Sea he looked at, but for a second Jumper saw there the glittering blue of the Kyrene Channel where he had watched ship after brave ship die a few months before. 'Yes,' he said, far away, 'if I never do nothing else I got three of them bleeders.'

He swung himself into the seat and strapped himself into the gun harness. His horny, brown seaman's hand reached out for the trigger and he fired a short burst. The long, black cannon jerked and punched at his solid shoulders like a road drill. He stopped and turned his head.

'That was nice while it lasted, as the bishop said to the actress,' he grinned.

'Do another burst!' said Wilsher, fascinated. Here was the real thing, hard and potent, the sure tongue of war itself.

'What, twice a night at my age!' said Jumper. 'No, mate. This ammo's scarce. Still, who knows, I might get the chance to shoot at something real again one of these days—not in this clapped-out, two-funnelled bastard, though.'

Up in the cold sky the bombers were forming up. As they flew swiftly from cloud to cloud through the pale spring sunshine they looked like long-necked geese rising from the shadowy saltings. They formed in line astern and the leader peeled off into his dive.

Almost at deck level he pulled out and came for them, tearing flat out for the maw of the guns. Jumper swung the Oerlikon towards the deadly shape and drew a bead upon it. He stopped being Uncle Jumper then and became a professional killer. 'This is where I come in,' he said.

The plane drew on, larger and larger, until, with a shattering roar it lifted over them, the dark shadow of its wings enveloping them for a split second like an omen of disaster, as a man will suddenly start and say, 'Someone just walked over my grave.' One by one the others followed, making their impotent passes at the old virgin cruiser.

'It's always the same,' grumbled Jumper. 'All make-believe, no action, nothing real. Nothing ever happens.'

But that afternoon something did happen, something which marked that day as a turning point in all their lives, a time of terrible portent.

The last two aircraft made their attacks simultaneously. They came in low, dropped their imaginary torpedoes from a height at which, in the real thing, they would have felt the splash in their faces, and roared over the ship, the backwash of their engines racketing along her decks. Once clear of the trajectory of her guns they banked away.

But in their inexperience the young pilots turned towards

each other. Before the horrified eyes of the boys on the training cruiser they collided.

The shuddering, smashing shock seemed to rock the ship, so great was the impact on their minds. The two planes burst apart in a roar of flame and dropped like great spent fireworks into the hissing, smoking sea. The grey water closed on them and quenched their fire.

Silence, a moment's vacuum, followed as the horror of the sight burst full upon them. Shocked and sick, they stared at the patches of burning oil and petrol.

For the cadets, it was their first sight of violence and death. Like the first sight of an enemy's smoke in the mirror of sky and sea, the shock stirred them for the first time into an awareness of what they were about, of war and the sterner purpose upon which they were embarked for life or death.

For them, and for the whole ship, nothing was ever quite the same from that moment on. The crash was like a flame, a first flicker in a slowly but relentless mounting train of violence which seemed to have awakened in the old ship's dry bones. Afterwards it seemed to them to have begun when the new captain came on that day of fog in Rosyth, with his ideas of turning a mob of irresponsible boys into fighting sailors, of taking placid old *Connie* into the very heart of the fire.

CHAPTER SEVEN

'ALL guns with semi-armour piercing shell load load load . . !'

Moore's voice trembled as he passed on the order from the Gunnery Officer to 'A' gun's crew of frightened cadets.

It was the climax of all the theory which the Gunner, Jumper and the other instructors had shot at them throughout the past weeks.

It was dramatic as well as complicated and frightening. Team by team, they took their places round the gun, layer, trainer, breech-worker, telephone operator and the rest, and went through the motions of firing a live round out of the long barrel of the big gun which sat in its splinter shield on *Constant*'s fo'c'sle like an ageing dragon breathing fire and smoke. It was the real thing this time—except that there was nothing real to fire at, no enemies for the dragon to scorch with its revolting breath.

It was, for once, a bright blue and gold afternoon, reminding the old hands of the Mediterranean. The cadets had been prepared for their ordeal by lectures in the morning on the anatomy of the fearsome weapon.

The Gunner sketched an elaborate breakdown of the six-inch gun. He told them how the recoil system attached to the bottom of the fixed cradle in which the big gun moved absorbed the tremendous berserk kick of the recoil and slowed it down to a controllable fury; how the run-out spring on the top of the cradle, compressed to a fierce, crouching potency by the recoil, struck back and returned the gun to its firing position. He showed them the intracacies of the huge breech, he described the electrical circuits, main and auxiliary, which supplied power to fire the gun. He spoke of mushroom heads, vent stalks and the like, images which suggested the delicate physiognomy of a flowering plant rather than the great champing jaw of brass and steel which was the breech. He touched on the B.M. lever, the great arm which, in the breech-worker's hands, wrenched the breech-block backwards out of that great jaw so that it vomited stinking cordite fumes. He illustrated the function of electric and percussion locks, of obturator pads and vent sealing tubes and box-slides and listed the four different ways of making the gun fire.

When he had finished, he quizzed them mercilessly on all these fearsome complexities, second nature to him long since, until they were bruised, battered and thoroughly blinded by the science of it all.

'Of course,' he said, 'this is a very simple type of gun, obsolete by modern standards, crude compared with a twin six-inch gun turret like you get on a modern cruiser like the *Ajax* or the *Achilles. They* were able to put paid to the *Graf Spee* with the six-inch guns they had, but it would be a pretty poor lookout for you if you were to run across a pocket battleship with this old kind that we've got. They were all right for the First World War and did a lot of good work then. As a matter of interest I was gun captain on a six-inch just like these at the Dogger Bank battle. I'm an old man now and that was a long, long time ago. All I hope is that you fight your guns as well as the lads did then, when the time comes.'

He looked at them and shook his head slowly. It was a visible sign of 'no confidence'. Then he went on with the main thread of his discourse and explained how the charge, a silken bag of cordite, ignited by a flash, exploded into a jet of gas which punched the shell, spinning at high speed up its spiral grooves inside the barrel, out of the gun.

They were given a list of all the different jobs at the gun and told to learn them by heart, 'because you'll all have to take your turn this afternoon'. After that they had an uneasy lunch.

This was the theory, the bare bones of the thing they were going to do in reality out on the bland and gently heaving fo'c'sle. It was the first serious piece of practice they had been called on to do, and the one which would bring them nearest to the smoke and noise and terror of a real naval battle.

'We'll probably never even see a six-inch gun again after this, let alone be asked to fire one in action,' said McCutchen, the know-all. 'It's a bloody load of flannel.'

He and Moore were cooks of the mess again, although after their performance on this memorable day of the shoot it was unlikely that they would ever be allowed to touch the food again. They had concocted a stew, which was just edible, and as a special treat they had prepared apple pie—a carefully folded envelope of dough with crudely sliced wedges of apple inside. Proudly they marched their creation in its tin to the galley to be baked in the big oven.

It wasn't until they had almost chewed away their front teeth on the muscular stew that Moore, his mind preoccupied uneasily with B.M. levers and obturator pads, suddenly remembered. . . .

'God! The apple pie!'

The blackened thing which they brought back to the mess was received in silence. Then . . .

'Cooks? You couldn't boil water!' said Jumper in disgust. He picked up the grim burnt offering, and pulling back his arm like a baseball pitcher, hurled it at the bulkhead. There was a dull, metallic sort of thud and the petrified pie dropped to the deck—intact.

'Was you thinking of using it this afternoon—instead of a projie?' he asked. 'It's harder than bleeding armour-piercing!'

Everybody beat on the table with spoons and forks and plates and reviled the wretched cooks. . . .

'You couldn't boil an egg!'

'Make 'em eat it!'

There was so much noise that Lieutenant Sample, the Assistant Divisional Officer, hurried down from the bridge all prepared to stamp out mutiny. When he had restored a sullen order to the mess he was told the cause of the fracas. He looked at the object in the tin, stroked his beard and shook his head sympathetically. 'I should nail it to the mast as a ghastly warning if I were you,' he said.

'Couldn't get a nail through it, sir,' said Jumper gloomily.

He was still brooding over the disaster when he put them

through their drill on the gun, and the memory made him crack the whip all the harder.

'Come on, you shower of spit! Get bloody weaving then!' he snarled at them as they doubled about their jobs. 'Come on now, slap it about a bit! The *Von* bleeding *Scheer* is out there about to open fire, so take it on the double! Thank Christ she isn't, that's all I can say, and thank the Lord for the bleeding Army! As you were!'

He glared suspiciously about him. 'Where's the Honourable? Gone to Lyons? Always bleeding adrift, that half-hard son of a carrier. I'll have his guts for a necktie when he shows up.'

But the Honourable Guy did not show up. Dishevelled and bewildered, the rest of the class went on with its relentless charade.

'Gun's crew close up!' It was the cue for the curtain to go up.

'Exercise action!' One man removed the housing stop and elevated the gun, whirling his little handwheel madly. Another, the breech-worker, opened the breech to check that the bore was clear. A third removed the tompion blocking the muzzle, another saw to the fitting of the telescopes, while others removed the securing chains and cleared the ammunition hoists.

'Gun well!' The range-taker, sitting petrified in his harness of headphones and mouthpiece under the lee of the splinter shield, plugged into the mounting like an electric light bulb into its socket, had to be kicked to make his report. This was the signal for number three to get tub and rammer, numbers five and seven the heavy one-hundred-pound shells, six and eight two cartridges, and the breech-worker, number two, a belt of tubes—the tiny electric charges which actually touched off the cordite—and a vent tool.

''A' gun closed up, cleared away, bore clear!'

They were ready for action, in theory at any rate.

'Change round!' At the double, tripping over eye bolts, colliding with each other, the team altered their positions at the gun so that everyone should have his turn at each different job. Jumper rolled his eyes in disgust at the sloppiness of their performance.

'All guns line up!'

Frantically the pointers on the dials at the gun were lined up with those repeating the director tower's range, bearing and elevation. Layer and trainer swung their hand wheels desperately.

'Receivers correct.' The trainer reported his training receiver correct, the breech-worker closed the interceptor mechanism which closed the firing circuit and burned the 'gun-ready' lamp in the transmitting station. The fire gong sounded.

'"A" gun circuits correct.' The breech-worker opened the interceptor once more, breaking the firing circuit.

They were still a long way from firing a live shell for the first time. It wasn't just a case of aiming and pulling a trigger. They were beginning to find that out.

There were many ways of making the gun fire efficiently, different chains of cause and effect which could be used in different situations, normal methods as well as those which could be resorted to in an emergency.

A modern shoot by six-inch guns was normally controlled and operated electrically, they were told, by the crew of the director up on the foremast above the bridge, where the control officer sat in command, with his layer operating the master trigger which fired the guns. The guns' crews were mere puppets who followed his motions so that the guns delivered a crashing broadside in response to the command 'Salvoes!', all the guns barking together as one. But the same guns could also be controlled and directed locally at each gun by the officer of the quarters, in which case they fired independently of one another. The cadets would be told something of this officer's job later on. At the moment they had far too much on their hands simply trying to give a poor imitation of a gun's crew. In this case the actual firing process was still normally done electrically.

They tested the two methods, both with the main and the auxiliary electrical circuits. Gradually they picked up a little speed and confidence, and began to go through the motion as if they knew what they were doing....

'With gun main fire a tube!' That was old Jan's acid bark.

'Switch to gunlayer!'

'Contact to main!'

The two shouts came almost simultaneously from two of the cadets at the gun. The breech-worker inserted the tiny tube, closed the interceptor and yelled, 'Tube inserted ready!' He slightly spoiled the effort by allowing his voice to crack on the high note, but the meaning was there.

'Fire!'

Old Jan might have been back at Jutland again, steaming hard through the smoke and geysers of boiling spray towards the winking gun flashes of Von Scheer's battle-cruisers. A sudden breeze whipped his hard, resolute old seaman's face and stood his jacket lapel up on end. It was a breeze that had gun-smoke in it and the stinging salt from all the oceans, all the weathers of the world. This was a long time, a long stretch of imagination away from Jutland and the Dogger Bank, but it was still his duty and he did it to the very utmost of his skill and ability.

'By gun main tube fired!' shouted the gun captain hoarsely.

'Very good,' crackled Jan. 'All guns test director circuits. With auxiliary test director circuits.'

'Tube inserted!'

'Range clear.'

Number two closed the interceptor. 'Ready.'

'Fire!'

'With auxiliary director circuits correct.'

'Very good. With main test director circuits.'

After an hour of this they reasembled a reasonably well-trained ballet, or at least they had the makings of one. Then at last came the real thing. . . .

'All guns with semi-armour piercing shell load load load!'

They were too hot and anxious to please him to notice the hollowness of Jan's 'Enemy in sight!' but swung instantly into their routine. Number two, unmindful now of a blue face and a sense of failure, snapped to and unmasked the vent, inserted a tube and shouted:

'Half cock!' The range taker shouted range and direction, layer and trainer swung the gun and:

'Salvoes!'

'Layer on!'

'Trainer on!'

The poet slammed the interceptor shut, closing the circuit linking the firing mechanism at the gun with the layer's master trigger up in the director. The gun was at the ready. Too busy now to be frightened of the yellow, semi-armour piercing live shell which lay in the gun. . . .

'Fire!'

The layer pulled the trigger. There was a nightmare, shattering roar as if every single atom in the universe had ruptured itself at the same time. The great bulk of the gun lunged madly back at them like a berserk railway engine. The gun had been trained across to starboard and the shell went gyrating in the direction of an empty horizon.

It was this particular moment which the Honourable Guy had chosen to rejoin his class. One hour adrift, he ran under the starboard wing of the bridge and burst out on to the naked plain of the fo'c'sle—just in time to come face to face with the burning, blinding gush of flame from the black mouth of the gun and have the white-hot ram of thunder skewered through his eardrum.

He reeled, screaming, the blood gushing from ears and nose, his head a roaring explosion of pain, his eyes slashed and ripped by barbs of fire. He fell to his knees on the deck, his hands to his face, moaning terribly in pain and fear and shock.

They half-led, half-carried him, stumbling and crying in shock, below to the coolness of the sick bay. The pain roared in his head and scourged his eyes like a surging wash of vitriol. But soon the roaring stopped and there was only silence, silence and the coolness of sheets, silence and utter blackness. . . . With white, unbelieving faces they watched him as his blundering fingers explored a new world of linen and serge and flesh, like children starting on a strange journey in the dark, trembling and fluttering like frightened girls, barking their joints on the side of the cot, dancing like macabre dolls to a moaning, hopeless tune as, with dawning horror, the boy began to know that he was deaf and blind.

CHAPTER EIGHT

THERE was no more gun practice. Nelson division secured and went below, as *Constant* made all speed to rush the injured boy to the naval hospital at Rosyth.

It was on this mercy run that the old ship gave of her very best. She had never thought to see twenty-five knots again, but she did it this day.

Steaming flat out through the shimmer of the sea she was a taut ship in every line of her. White water peeled from her stem, and her rigging sang in the green wind. She cut a dash that day and looked like the gleam in her architect's eye—a fast ship, a dashing sailor with a jut to her chin and white wings of foam at her heels.

Her rivets danced in their holes, her funnels were red hot and the deck around them warm through the thin soles of pusser's slippers.

'We're off, and so are the bookies,' said Jumper Cross, 'but we're after 'em and when we catch 'em will we not give 'em a doin'! She'll burst a bleedin' blood vessel at this rate!'

For years she had cruised and patrolled the wide, peaceful oceans in idleness. Now those lion-hearted engines which Tyneside had fitted into her so long ago did what they had been built to do and sent her flying. Asleep for so long, old *Connie* was awake now, caught up in that murmuring tide of violence which had started four weeks ago, it seemed, and roared to high watermark in this afternoon's brutal climax.

She reached Rosyth and Stott was put ashore. They never saw him again.

Then the *Constant,* heartless slut, turned her back on futility and steamed off, bottom waggling in white water, nose held high and stepping over the slapping waves like the fast madam she had suddenly become.

Out at sea, training went on as before. Nelson division had seen what fighting a gun was like. Now they were shown how to control all the effort and urge of men and machinery and Direct it to its object—hurting the enemy.

Sub-Lieutenant James, the very new young R.N.V.R. officer, fresh from H.M.S. *Excellent* at Whale Island and the officers' training establishment at *King Alfred*, took the preliminary lecture. Fire control was his sweetheart now, he had fallen in love with her aloof perfection at *Excellent*.

James, the cadets of Nelson division and the captain himself were all contemporaries in *Constant*. They had all joined her on that same foggy, somehow ominous day at Rosyth nearly four weeks ago, all young men, all new to the ship, all untried in her. Subby remembered the day with a shudder, even now. Fresh and green as the grass in the meadow, smarting and sulking under the imaginary injustice which had sent him, the best gunner in his division at *King Alfred*, to an old, worn-out training cruiser, he had been plunged straight away in the routine and responsibility of assistant to the officer of the day, and Dickinson had given him a bad time. First, the boat bringing the new class of cadets to the ship had been overdue, then the new captain's boat. They had been worried, and young James had pictured a frail launch run down in the fog and drowning men in that icy water. . . .

Gradually he had become more reconciled to his lot, although it never once occurred to him that he had been sent to help train the new boys because of his outstanding qualities, and not in spite of them. It would have been thoroughly bad for him if he had realised this, for he had been very sure of himself when he left *King Alfred* in such a blaze of glory, and any further accolades might have overbalanced his precariously poised ego. As it was, his sense of having been found wanting after all made him knuckle down to the hard, humdrum realities of the job he had. *Constant* was good for his soul, though he did not know it. 'Glory' is a big word, but it lay shining there in Subby's smouldering ambition. He thought he would never get it in the *Constant*.

'The officer of the quarters takes charge of a section of the ship's armament,' he said firmly. 'Is that clear?'

He knew it by heart and he understood what he was saying. But he could not look them all in the eye and say '*I* have been an officer of the quarters in battle, *I* have taken charge of a section of the ship's armament.' He felt ashamed every time he heard himself speak the words.

'He makes sure of the safety and efficiency of all weapons under his charge and of all ammunition, shell rooms, magazines and all the machinery attached to his quarters. . . .' *They know I'm just a greenhorn, not much better than themselves. I can see it in their faces. They resent me. They think I'm coming it over them.*

'. . . takes care of explosives, carries out the periodical inspection and test af all ammunition and guns . . .' *That's something I have done. You don't have to have been in action to have done that. But what's the point in testing* Connie's *guns*?

'. . . organises guns' crews, supply parties, magazine crews . . .' He looked round at the faces of his class again as he spoke and wondered how on earth even the Gunner himself could make these helpless babes in arms into guns' crews and the rest. He doubted them and at the same time sympathised with their uneasy state of being—neither rating nor officer, neither man nor boy. He knew from his own experience what they felt—even the cocksure ones and the gong-polishers, who only thought of the glamour of the uniform. He'd been through all that himself. But now he was beginning to learn the reality behind an officer's uniform. His self-confidence had been shaken, but not shattered, by this awareness which the *Constant* had given him, because at least he had the theory by rote and loved his trade.

'. . . is in charge of a gun or guns during firing practice . . .' I've had some of that, he thought. It's just a routine, a formal dance. Once you've learnt it, it stays learnt, with no surprises, no variations and no call for original thought.

'. . . . or in action.' That was the phrase which rang like a fire-gong, lit up like a gun-ready lamp. It was a pounding heart and a surge of soul, a longing to conquer set against a ground base of fear. *I can do it. Just give me the chance.*

When the lecture was over he went back to his cabin and stared once more at the books along the little shelf, the *Officer of the Quarters' Handbook, Gunnery Pocket Book, Handbook on Guns and Mountings*. For the umpteenth time he took down and read through A.F.O. 1024-5/41, *Instructions on Care and Maintenance*, in preparation for the afternoon lecture.

The Gunner himself sat in on the afternoon session. He sat down in an empty desk at the back of the classroom, and James knew he was on trial as much as the cadets, like a student teacher in front of a sullen Lower Fourth.

'All right,' said Jan. 'Now I want to see what you've learnt. How often must the officer of the quarters carry out his inspection of magazines and shell rooms?' Like a canny schoolmaster, he always asked the question first so that no one knew who would have to answer it. He looked grimly round him at the anxious faces. 'Yes? You.' He nodded at his victim.

'Every twenty-four hours, sir.'

'Correct. What sort of oil should be used in preserving fuses? Moore?'

The poet jumped, startled. 'Oil, sir?'

'Oil.'

Then he remembered. He'd written it down in his little book. It was a catch question with a funny answer. 'You don't use oil, sir. You use Cooper's Grease.'

'Correct.' Old Jan barked the word like a salvo. 'Now, what would you do with the B.L. charge after the round has been fired?' he said. 'And I don't want no rude answers neither.' Another catch question. He nodded at McCutchen, who grinned and smirked a little. You couldn't catch Jack McCatchen with an easy one like that. There were no flies on him, he had it all weighed off.

'I wouldn't do anything with it, sir,' he said and paused returning the ball to Jan's court.

'Oh?' croaked the Gunner's voice. 'You'd just leave it in the breech then?' *Cocky young bastard. These kids think they know all the answers—kids of their age always do. Always looking in the mirror to admire themselves. Every brat who's found out what his balls are for thinks he's discovered the secret of life. Boys! I've spit 'em!*

'No, sir,' said McCutchen. 'There wouldn't be anything *left* in the breech, sir, not with unfixed B.L. ammunition. The charge is destroyed, sir.'

'Correct. All right, sub-lieutenant, carry on. But...' He jerked to his feet and made them all look at him by the sheer force of his personality. 'There's just one thing I want to impress on you. It's all very clever to learn what's in the books. It's very nice to be able to stand up and say "The such-and-such a gun fires so many rounds a minute, sir", and think that's all there is to it. But fighting a ship in a real battle at sea isn't like doing your exams at school. You've left all that sort of thing behind now. This is life, no more skylarks now, and you're on your own.

'You've got to be able to put all this book work into practice when it's called for. That's what counts. You've left school now, you're going to be officers and tell men what to do. And if you go and tell them the wrong thing or lose your nerve just because the hogwash is a bit rough or somebody's heaving bricks at you—then it isn't like losing that scholarship or the new bike your dad promised you if you passed—it's your life, and the lives of all the men in your charge. All right, carry on, please.' He stared at Subby.

There was a big silence after he had gone. That was meant for me as well, thought James. The sour old bastard, he hates my guts. He thinks I'm bloody useless, and all the other V.R.'s as well. He thinks we're amateurs playing at war. The old sod's past it, he's in his dotage and he doesn't like to see young chaps coming up to take over from him.

Outside in the passageway Jan Price thought, A wonderful bloody pep-talk! And what bloody good will it do? What good will a clapped-out old ship and a few bomb-happy bastards like me do? We might as well be loafing in Pompey Barracks drinking tea. What good did talking ever do for cocky ignorant kids? I talked to my own boy like that once and I might as well have saved my breath. It's not talking that does it. It's action that finds 'em out—like that silly young sod yesterday running right in front of the muzzle. And they want to put stupid young idiots like that in charge of ships and men!

Nevertheless he was back in the classroom himself an hour later to talk a lot more.

'The enemy's speed, direction of wind, inclination and range, are estimated by the rate officer in the control position,' he crackled, 'and passed down to the transmitting station.' Later they all went down to *Constant*'s own transmitting station and saw for themselves the complex machinery which, like an electrical or mechanical brain, helped to turn information from the director into action at the guns.

'We're below the water line here,' said Jan. 'The T.S. is the brain of the ship and is always located as far from harm's way as possible.' He pointed to the dials which filled the little cell of the T.S.

'This one is called the Dumaresq. On there is put the ship's speed, the bearing of the enemy and his estimated speed, and the inclination—that's the angle between the line of sight from you to him and his fore and aft line—and it works out your rate—opening or closing in three figures—and deflection—the angle to left or right of the line of sight—for you. The deflection is passed to the director up aloft, which is a master gunsight clear of smoke and spray, and the range is passed there as well as soon as the Vickers range clock *here* has worked it out from the rate. Then the director transmits all the necessary information to the receivers at the gun. The guns line up with the director—you've all done that so you ought to know what I'm talking about—and wait for the order to fire. Well, that's roughly the chain of control. Of course there are corrections coming through all the time from the spotting officer aloft. All right, now we shall be having a dummy run. I want ten of you to man the T.S. and the rest in the director.'

In company with Rodney division, the class immediately junior to them providing the gun's crew this time, the nervous Nelsons played at being a director's and a transmitting station's crew.

McCutchen, suddenly fearful again with his terror of heights, felt sick when he was detailed off as director layer. The director was not as high as the yardarm at *Ganges*, but it was still a terrifying peak to McCutchen. Furtively he canvassed the T.S. crew and managed to exchange places with the Dumaresq operator without being noticed.

Wilsher found himself spotting officer. He knew the theory and longed to do well this afternoon. This time they shot at a target towed, at a very great distance, by a tug, which even so took its life in its hands.

The first shot went wide to the left of the target and the men on the tug looked at each other in some alarm. Some of them actually felt spray on their faces from the fountain kicked up by the shell.

Wilsher knew he had to pull the gun round to the right. He wanted to say, 'Right two hundred!' but by the time his agonised vocal chords could function the gunner had had time to say:

'And what do you think Jerry is doing all this time? Do you think he's waiting for us to have another go? Do you know the Germans are the best gunners in the world? Do you realise they'd have put about three salvoes into us by now? Do you? *Do* you? Say something if it's only good-bye—and believe me that's all you'd be able to say by now if that was the *Hipper* out there or the *Prinz Eugen*!'

Miserable and sick at heart, the wretched boy stumbled on. Jan did not spare him. If he could not correct his guns quickly he was useless. That was all there was to it.

When the next cadet took over he was lucky. His first shot fell close to the target, but short. The next pitched about the same distance away on the other side. A straddle.

'Down one hundred!' he said quickly. The next round shattered the target. Old Jan grunted.

'Now you've got to learn how to do that every time,' he said.

Moore, in the T.S., was very unhappy. Down here in the fetid bowels of the ship, the motion seemed twice as violent and his stomach had begun to rise, so that he saw the pointers on the dial in front of him through a bilious haze. He thought how awful it would be down here in a real battle, being sick from heat and fumes and nausea, although none of that would be as bad as the fear of what might happen if a torpedo struck the ship's thin flanks and they were trapped here by fire or rising water.... The others might have been feeling bad too, but they did not have Moore's imagination....

'Jumper,' he said weakly, 'I can't stand it down here, I want to go on deck. I can't stand this.'

'You've got to stand it, lad,' said the leading hand. 'You're at action stations now. If you deserted your post now you might sink the ship. Come on, chop chop, grab that handle!'

Groaning, the poet turned back to the jazzing face of the dial. By and by, he began to feel a little clearer and the wave of nausea retreated to a manageable position. But he was glad to get on deck and draw in lungful after lungful of harsh, salt air.

'Well, I know one thing,' he said fervently, 'I never want to go in submarines!'

'Don't worry, mate,' said Jumper, 'I can't see 'em asking you. You'll be lucky if they let you go on the Gosport ferry.'

That night *Constant* crept her way back to the Forth in thick fog.

The cadets were at their watchkeeping stations on the guns, on the bridge and on lookout duty. In these conditions their duties were very real and a genuine responsibility for the safety of the ship rested upon their shoulders.

'Who's on masthead lookout?' asked the captain.

'Wilsher, sir,' said Dickinson.

'The boy that stutters?' said the captain doubtfully.

'Yes, sir.'

'Is that wise?'

'He's got to learn, sir.'

'All right.'

They could hardly be more anxious than the masthead lookout himself, rolling in his airborne sentry box through crazy parabolas in the weird, eerie half darkness up where the fog thinned out into banks and shoals and nightmare shapes, with livid, moonlit lagoons between them.

There were moaning sirens all around them, calling like lost, damned souls.

Suddenly there was a loud booming blare from close ahead.

From out of the darkness above the fog came, like some giant periscope, the truck of a mast.

In the *Constant* only one man saw it. Without a second thought Wilsher bent to the voicepipe, eyes on the masthead, estimating the direction of the other vessel. Heart beating wildly, he shouted:

'Hard-a-starboard! Hard-a-starboard!'

Completely blind, trusting in the boy's judgment of the position because he had no choice, the captain passed the order to the wheelhouse.

Slowly, agonisingly, the *Constant*'s head began to swing.

On the bridge, on the fo'c'sle, they could see a great steel side and a bridge and upperworks towering over them....

Just as the cruiser's bow seemed about to bite into the huge bulk of the other ship, she seemed to veer away. Awed and silent, like sailors staring at the sheer and terrible tower of an iceberg, they watched the great mass of the aircraft carrier plunge out of the night down their side, then vanish again into the greyness of the fog.

Five minutes later Wilsher was on the bridge. The captain told him that he had almost certainly saved the ship.

'Thank you, sir,' said the boy. There was a new light in his eyes and a ring in his voice that had not been there before. He did not stutter.

'Frankly, I was doubtful whether you should be up there at all in these conditions,' said Harker, 'but you've made it quite obvious that I was wrong. You never hesitated for a second in assuming complete command of the ship. How did you manage to get your words out now, when you usually trip headlong over them?'

'I, well, it was simply a question of having to, sir,' said Wilsher.

The incident had shaken them all, and it may have been because of this that the accident happened....

As *Constant* steamed slowly down the Forth, then went astern to come to anchor, the cadets of Nelson division had gone to their positions for entering harbour on the fo'c'sle.

As the cruiser idled to a stop, the captain shouted:

'Let go for'ard!'

Moore swung his hammer, knocked the pin from the Blake slip which alone held the menacing weight of anchor and cable, and instantly the thick grey links began to clang and roar over the deck and down through the naval pipe. Next moment there was a terrible scream.

The boy standing next to Moore had not noticed the poet's quick action as he swung the hammer to knock away the slip. He was a highly-strung boy and the sudden clangour of berserk cable made him jump.

He turned, lost his balance and stepped right into the savage cable.

Instantly he was wrenched off his feet, one foot jammed in a link of chain, and hurled across the deck towards the yawning mouth of the navel pipe.

Dickinson, standing near the navel pipe, reacted first. A second before the petty officer in charge of the cable holder jammed on his screaming brakes, the divisional officer threw himself in a rugger tackle at the body of the cadet.

His action saved the boy from being mangled in the navel pipe. Dickinson's grip on his body was enough to jerk him free of the cable.

Shocked and anxious to help, everyone rushed to the pair sprawled on the deck. The squeamish ones turned away at once and one or two went to the rail to be sick when they saw what the cable had done to the boy's foot. . . .

Unconscious, white and rigid with shock, the cadet was carried below, the second customer for the sick bay in two days.

'What's got into the bloody ship?' everyone asked. 'What's gone wrong?'

'It's the new skipper,' said someone. 'He's got a bloody jinx on him.'

'He's trying to force the pace too much,' said an officer, putting the same feeling into different words. 'He thinks he's still got a destroyer. Don't worry, he'll kill us all yet.'

CHAPTER NINE

NEXT day the cadets went on a short week-end leave in Edinburgh. They were always glad to go. There they could relax and forget the *Constant*—the filthy washplace, the herrings-in, the sweat of the syllabus, the worry of failure—there they could wallow like happy pigs in the luxury of a hot bath at the Y.M.C.A., followed by tea with cream cakes at the Balmoral in Princes Street and an evening in the pub or at the pictures. There they could forget what had happened to Guy Stott and to the wretched lad on the previous afternoon—try to shut out the sound of that scream.

Dickinson stayed on board. He seldom went ashore, now that there was never anyone to meet him. And if he stayed in his cabin there was no one to write home to and no home to go to anywhere in the world for him any more. He was left alone with his photographs and his bitter memories.

The Gunner was officer of the day. Like Dickinson he had no wish, no reason to go ashore, and he stayed in the ship like a hurt old badger withdrawing into his hole in the earth. He stayed there all alone, and there were never any visitors from other ships, because the people that might have visited him were all dead. And he had no son any more to write to.

He was very surprised, therefore, and a little suspicious, when the quartermaster knocked on his cabin door and told him that there was an officer asking for him at the gangway.

'It's an R.A.F. officer, sir,' said the leading hand, 'a pilot officer, I think.'

'All right,' said old Jan, 'I'll come up.'

When he got on deck he shaded his eyes from the sudden bleak brilliance of the afternoon sun and looked towards the top of the gangway.

Sure enough there was a young R.A.F. officer standing there. Jan blinked and puckered up his tired old face.

'Hello, Dad,' said the young man.

'Good God!' said the Gunner. 'What the hell are you doing here?'

'I'm on my way up north,' said the pilot, 'and I heard the ship was in. I've only got half an hour but . . . well, we haven't seen each other for a long time, have we?'

'No, not for a long time, son,' said Jan. He didn't know what to do or say. He had taken his stand once, he had said all he thought he would ever say then to the boy who had been his son. But this strange young man with the pilot's wings on his pale blue tunic did not look like his son, not like that boy he had turned away from the door so long ago.

'You . . . I . . .' his harsh old voice broke suddenly and tears welled up into his eyes. 'I'm glad to see you, son,' he said huskily, 'I'm glad to see you. It's been a long time.'

'That's my fault,' said the boy, 'after what I did. You did me a good turn when you kicked me out.'

'No,' said his father. 'No, son, I shouldn't have done that. I was wrong. I didn't even give you a chance to defend yourself. Come on now, come on below and tell me all about yourself.'

'Well, I knocked about a bit after that business,' said young Price, when they were seated below in the Gunner's bare little cabin, 'drifting from one job to another and not doing any of 'em very well, and then the war came and, well, the Air Force wasn't quite so particular as the Navy was. They didn't think I was quite as bad as all that and, well, here I am.'

'Yes, and you've got your wings, too,' said Jan. He was smiling now, there was new life in him, he had got his son back and he was proud of him in his uniform, proud of the man he had become after all. Then he frowned as he remembered something from the bad old days.

'That girl,' he said hesitantly. 'Did you . . .'

'That was one of the things everybody misunderstood, Dad,' he said. 'It wasn't the way they said at all. As a matter of fact we got married. We've got a kid now, a boy. You're a grandad. He's three next month. Looks just like you.'

'A son!' The old man could hardly speak, his cup was so full. All these years he had lived in silence and bitterness alone and now here was all the warmth of life flooding back to him.

'Look, here he is!' Before long he was looking at snapshots of a smiling girl and the baby, his grandson, she held so proudly in her arms.

'You see, we loved each other, Dad, we wanted to get married. I hated Dartmouth and so did she. I only pinched that money because I was desperate and couldn't think straight. I thought that if I did that they'd *have* to chuck me out.'

'Somehow I knew it wasn't you, not really my son, to do a thing like that,' said the Gunner, happier than he could have believed possible. 'That's why I was so hurt. But there must have been a lot I didn't understand.'

'Well, you were always away and then mother was always ill. We were never together as a family, were we?'

'Well, we're a family now, any road,' said the Gunner. 'Here, let me look at those snaps again. A grandad! Oh my! I can't believe it, I just can't believe it!'

Soon it was time for him to go. 'We're going up north to train on Beaufort's—torpedo dropping,' he said.

'Torpedo dropping! Here, you leave that to the Navy; we don't want none of you smart boys taking away our jobs!' said Jan. 'I might get up to see you from here, then.'

'Or I might be able to wangle a crafty forty-eight and come down here again,' said his son. 'Anyway, it's been terrific seeing you again, Dad.'

'Oh, you don't know what it's meant to me, son,' said the Gunner. 'You can't have any idea.'

'Well, so long, Dad.'

'Bye-bye, lad,' said Jan. 'And I'll look forward to seeing you—and the wife and kiddie—soon.'

As young Price went over the side Dickinson came up the ladder from below.

'Hello, Guns,' he said. 'I'm just going ashore for a short spell to see that boy in hospital. Poor young devil. What do we put him down as—war casualty?'

'That's about it, sir,' said Jan. He wanted to say, 'That was my son just now, the Air Force officer,' but he thought perhaps it might be a tactless remark. He knew about Dickinson's own son and did not want to rub in his newly-found happiness.

Dickinson walked stiffly down the brow to the dock and made for the dockyard gates. A chill breeze sidled shiftily through the dirty roadway and sighed in the coppice of stark black cranes, tumbling an old cigarette packet across his shoe. It was Saturday afternoon in Rosyth, forlorn fagend of a week which nobody from Shetland to Singapore had wanted, a week of boredom and bloodshed, misery and dirt, a week of war. And here was Lieutenant-Commander Dickinson, R.N., trudging through an empty dockland on the path of duty—always a rocky, uphill path towards a goal of pain and gall and bitterness. He strove, and all he strove for turned to pain and death. It was his profession to deal in death, of course, but others had not been weighed down with the cross of duty as he had, dark and bitter duty ending always in some crucifixion on a lonely hill. Death had struck him close, robbing him of loved ones and friends and leaving him utterly alone.

He climbed the hospital steps, his heart heavy, as ever. They had operated on the boy that morning, so it was unlikely that they would allow visitors so soon. Dickinson thought, I saved him, but for what? He's a young, active boy. Will he thank me, when he's stumbling about on crutches, watching his friends running, walking, playing—standing on their own feet? In a way he felt this as a responsibility, as if he had become a sort of god-parent in suffering to the crippled lad.

It's thwarted fatherhood, he thought. Just because Lance is gone and there's no one ... But there may be something I can do for him. He didn't die, like my son and that other boy long ago in the mutiny ... If only I had seen it sooner, if only I could have prevented it ... Prevented what? The whole war? The whole sickness of mankind? ... Poor children, and that's all they are, poor children. What did we do wrong? How did we get them into this? They can't stand up to this war, it's too great a cross for children to bear. We got them into it. We deserve to pay for that, and we have paid. And now there are only a handful of us left, and they, our sons, must pay for what we did—or for what we left undone. Dickinson was always close to prayer these days, but he had no God to pray to any more. He did not want God any more. He was through with folk tales. You could twist logic any way you wanted to prove the existence of a Power beyond human destiny, and everyone secretly craved the security of an omniscient, benevolent Father, but you couldn't twist the facts into a pattern of moonbeams. For Dickinson there was nothing to believe in any more, and nothing to live for. So he felt deeply sorry and concerned for the young men who came to the *Constant*. They were so eager and so full of hope, and they did not know how weak and foolish were all men, how empty and vain and meaningless the life they led. They thought they could fight a veteran's battle and win, they thought the struggle had an aim. They were pathetic in their ignorance, lambs in a cruel, savage world.

But in spite of his sick emptiness he contrived to go through the motions, to play a part in this hollow charade which signified nothing, to carry out his allotted duty to the best of his abilities. If he had stopped he would have died, simply ceased to be, for no man can live on the self alone, for there is no self separate from a man's action and desire. In Dickinson this action and desire, he imagined, had died to cold ashes. But there was a glow, deep down, unknown to him, a spark which he could not see waiting for feeling to breathe upon it and flame out. . . .

In the hospital he found what he had expected. The patient was doing well, although still suffering from shock. His foot had been amputated.

'By the way,' said the sister, 'his mother is here.'

'His mother?' He was surprised. Somehow he had assumed sole responsibility for the boy. 'So soon?'

'She hadn't far to come. She was rather upset, of course, and we put her in that room over there where she could be quiet and rest for a while. I don't know whether ... whether you would care to see her . . .?'

'Would it do any good, do you think?'

'Well, I think it might. She's all alone, poor girl, and she's had a terrible shock.'

'You don't think ... I mean, mightn't it remind her too much of ... what happened?'

'No, I don't think so. I rather think it would help her to know the facts. She seems to have the idea that there seems to have been some ... negligence, or that the boy was driven beyond his capacity. She's under great emotional stress, you know.'

'All right, I'll go in and see her,' said Dickinson reluctantly, 'but I shan't know what to say.'

He stood at the door for a moment, awkward, anxious, on the threshold of a delicate and hopeless errand. What could he say that would comfort the woman waiting inside? Dickinson paused, hand on the door knob, waiting.

Quickly he opened the door and went in. The woman sitting on the other side of the room staring out of the window turned her head and started to rise to her feet.

'Oh, please,' said Dickinson, putting his hand out impulsively to stop her, 'please don't get up.'

She looked at him without speaking for a second. Dickinson felt his heart thumping.

'Are you my son's commanding officer?' she said. She had a lovely voice, soft and slightly husky—probably with crying, he thought.

'Yes. I'm his divisional officer,' he said gently. 'I saw it happen.'

'Does it matter how it happened?' asked the boy's mother. Her face was very white.

'I thought ... I thought it might help if you knew....'

'All I know is that my son will never be able to walk properly again, that's all I want to know,' she said in a low voice. Again he thought what a beautiful voice it was. She is lovely with her grief; there are raw edges to her voice where tears had torn salt wounds.

He said, 'It isn't as bad as that.' His voice was gentle and his eyes searched her face and her beauty, caressing her womanliness.

'*It isn't as bad as that* ...' she mocked him. 'They've ...' Her voice quavered and he thought she was going to break down.

'They've taken his foot off. He's a cripple . . .' Her voice was rising. 'You let that happen to a young boy, you let that happen. . . . You should have taken more care of them. They are boys, not men—boys, and you let that happen to them!' She put her hands to her face and began to cry with tearing, wrenching sobs.

Dickinson stared at her. *You should have taken more care of them. They are boys, not men. . . .*

It hurt him, but he had been hurt before, whipped raw by the world. He had been hurt so much that he had fancied himself immune, punch-drunk with pain.

But all that was nothing compared with this accusation. *You should have taken more care of them.* This hurt him more than all the rest put together. What this woman had said had hurt him more than anything. He had thought he was mastering it, almost over it, but this woman had broken through and wounded him worse than ever before. He had thought he was dead to hurtful impressions, but this woman had roused him, first with her beauty and her womanliness, all made doubly strong by the heightened sexual bloom which grief paints upon a lovely woman. All the seductive shock of her had shaken him. She had touched him deeply and shocked his numb feelings awake. The emotion that was hidden deep, like a lava-flood in the silent earth, surged up and burst upon him. He came to life like a beaten lover, and his bitter, longing heart burst open like an old wound. She had stirred him, seduced him, first with her beauty that grief had made all naked for him to see, then with this angry, vicious insult like the venom of an outraged mistress. He moved towards her, his eyes angry.

'Yes,' he said, 'they are boys. They are boys whom we are trying to turn into men. They have wandered into a man's world, strayed like silly lambs into a jungle. They are lambs and we are teaching them to fight wolves. Do you think they can stay little boys for ever? They have to learn, they must be strong or there will be no world for them to live in. What do you want us to do? Tell them how nice everything is going to be in the best of possible worlds? Do you think the Germans will pity them because they are "only boys"? Good God! Your son has lost a foot! He isn't dead. He isn't dead, but I could give you a thousand names of men and boys who are dead and shattered much worse than your son, I could tell you that three-quarters of all the men who started this war at sea alive—fighting for you and your son and all the other little boys safe at home—are gone now! They are all dead, all the friends I knew, all of them, every one, all dead. I lost my own son at sea. He was a good boy but when he died he died like a man. He had learned that much and he died fighting a man's fight against this filthy, degrading thing that is trying to kill us all. He was eighteen years old, but he was a man, and he died like a man. Your son is lucky. My little boy was burned to death. I wish to God my son had been your son, *because he would be alive.*'

He stopped, utterly disgusted with himself. He had bared all his feelings to her. He had made his confession to her as to a priest or a wife.

She said quietly, 'Once when I was a little girl I got hysterical when I fell over and cut my knee, and my father twisted my arm to shock me out of it. I'm very sorry for what I said to you.'

'I did what I could for your son,' said Dickinson in an exhausted voice. 'I just managed to pull him away in time to stop him from being even more badly hurt. I am sorry I couldn't have done more.'

He was so humble and so drained of will that she wanted to comfort him. 'Please forget what I said and don't think any more about it,' she said. He looked up and saw the tender expression in her eyes. She's not like Frances, he thought, she's stronger than Frances was.

They stood and looked at each other, lost in their loneliness and pain, each wanting to move towards the other for comfort, each knowing it to be impossible.

'I was wondering,' said Dickinson haltingly, 'if you . . . do you have to stay here now?'

'They said I would not be able to see him until six o'clock this evening,' she said.

'It would do you good to get away from here till then,' he said gently.

'Perhaps it would,' she said.

'I was going to suggest that you might like to have tea with me in the town somewhere,' he said quietly, with a lift of eagerness in his voice.

'I should like to very much.' She smiled.

'Please forgive me,' said Dickinson. 'It was unforgivable—what I said just now. I lost control.'

'I deserved it. Now please take me out to tea and entertain me or I shall cry again,' she said.

They went to the Balmoral. As they were going into the café, three of the cadets from *Constant* passed them. Dickinson recognised Moore, McCutchen and Wilsher.

'Good afternoon, sir,' they chorused as they passed him. He nodded at them.

'Good God!' said McCutchen, when they had passed out of earshot, 'he actually smiled at us!'

'Were they from your ship?' she asked him, when they had found a table.

'Yes,' he said, 'they were three of my boys.'

She smiled at him. 'You are really fond of them all, aren't you?' she said.

'Yes, I suppose I am,' he said. 'I suppose, in a way, I'm trying to make up for my boy. But I don't have to show it, you know.'

'I think you would have liked my husband,' she said quietly. 'He went down in the *McKinley Bay*.'

Dickinson stared at her. 'Your husband died at sea?' he said. 'My God, and I said all that to you. . . .'

'Don't worry. It's what he would have said if he had been alive. He always used to say I was spoilt before he married me. It's because I was so alone after he was killed that I spent all my affection on Peter.'

'You are lucky to have your son,' he said. 'You see, I have no one now, I am completely alone.'

She caught her breath. 'Your wife . . . is she . . .'

He was staring at the tablecloth. 'My wife was always a highly strung person,' he said, 'and after Lance was born her health was bad. I was hardly ever at home and he was all she had to turn to. When the news came that he had been killed she must have felt that she couldn't face life any longer. She . . . did away with herself. I got the news at sea. I couldn't even get home to see her buried.'

'I am so very sorry,' she said.

'I'm afraid it's an old story and I don't come out of it very well,' he said.

'You mustn't say that,' she said. 'It was a terrible thing to happen.'

'And you? To lose your husband and then have this happen to your son?'

'We are both alone,' she said.

'Yes,' he said.

For a second they said nothing, but looked at each other.

Dickenson broke the silence. 'Well, I certainly haven't cheered you up much, have I? Where's that waitress?'

Afterwards they went back to the hospital together. They met the sister in the corridor.

'How is he, sister?' asked Dickinson.

It's as if he were the boy's father, thought the nurse quickly. She said, 'He's very much better. He's going to be all right now.' Her Scottish voice was warm and reassuring.

'Thank God,' said Dickinson. He felt her grip tighten on his arm.

He did not go in to see the boy himself, but left his mother to go to him. He said good-bye to her in the white corridor, with nurses bustling to and fro around them and a clatter of trolleys being wheeled swiftly through the wards.

'I'm glad he's going to get over the shock,' he said, not wanting to go. 'But he's going to need a lot of looking after.'

'He's going to need someone to show him that life can be worth living after all,' she said. 'Only a man can give that to him.'

Dickinson felt his heart pounding. 'I was thinking . . .' he began.

'Yes?' she said, looking up at him quickly.

'I . . . no, it was nothing,' he mumbled.

'Please tell me what you were going to say.'

'I wonder . . . if we could meet again some time soon?'

'I should like that very much,' she said, and his heart beat for joy. 'If you like, I'll write to you and let you know how Peter gets on.'

'Oh, would you?' He was eager and young.

'Good-bye.'

'Good-bye.'

He watched her walk off down the corridor until she turned a corner and was gone. Then he turned away and made his way back slowly to the ship. He felt a different man, a man with hope for the future.

But, staring out of the window of his first-class compartment at the ugly outskirts of Grantham, on his way to an appointment at the Admiralty which would change the face of the future for all of them, was the captain of the *Constant.*

The ship lay idle alongside the dockyard wall, silent and still as an empty house. Only a thread of smoke from the galley gave away the dormant life that lay smoking in her.

On a different horizon, a grey-green half light above another ocean, a thin column of funnel smoke like an Indian signal on the distant hills showed where another ship pursued her destiny deep in the grey salt saharas of the Atlantic. It was a destiny whose high noon was yet to come, the destiny of a ship called the *Kaiser Wilhelm.*

CHAPTER TEN

HARKER faced the senior officer across a vast, littered desk top. The grey-haired captain, a retired regular officer recalled to the Fleet on the outbreak of war, was sixty-five and looked it, making the captain of *Constant* seem a very young man indeed.

'Yes, I've read your report,' he said. 'It's a very forthright document, if I may say so. There are some quarters in which it wouldn't be at all popular.'

Harker, facing him squarely across the small wasteland of memos and the little pagoda of the captain's out tray, looked pugnacious.

'It wasn't meant to be *popular*, sir,' he said.

'No, well, we didn't expect anything less from you Harker,' said the older man with a smile. 'But it *is* hard hitting.'

'The situation calls for hard hitting, sir,' said Harker.

'As I see it, then,' said the senior officer, tilting back in his chair and staring at the ceiling, his fingers pressed delicately together, 'those young men are not getting enough sea-time.'

'That's about it, sir,' said Harker. 'On the whole, the sort of chap who used to come to the Fleet from a general service ship after, say twelve months *genuine* sea-time, perhaps even with a spell of real action to his name, turns out a good officer—within the limts of civilian entry, of course . . .'

'Quite so,' said the captain, smiling to himself.

'. . . because he's had the necessary backing of experience. I think I know what I'm talking about, sir. We had half a dozen very promising C.W. candidates in the *Killarney*, besides a couple of first-class chaps in the wardroom. They all went down with the ship. Now, of course, sir, I fully realise the impossibility of getting enough recruits from this source. In the light of the Navy's requirements some scheme of training on the present lines is obviously essential.'

'But you don't think at present it is being run on the right lines?' put in the other.

'No, sir, I do not,' said the young commander emphatically. 'I am all for taking short cuts when absolutely necessary—I don't think I've ever been considered a very orthodox type myself—*but*, and I feel very strongly about this, there are limits.'

'And the *Constant* has overstepped them?' The captain was wholly serious now. They were getting down to business.

'I think the amount of genuine sea experience is totally inadequate, sir,' said Harker. 'For ratings, perhaps—yes. For officer candidates—no. The classroom work and the practical instruction on deck is all very well—it's obviously more effective to use a ship for the job than a shore establishment—and I have no misgivings whatsoever about the efficiency and enthusiasm of my instructors—I've said as much in my report—but the point is that the whole of it could just as well be carried out alongside the wall. As for the sea experience, that consists of a few hours of playing at watchkeeping, most of which is spent in harbour and is in any case broken up by instruction. At no time are they given the chance to get the feel of whole days and nights of regular watchkeeping at sea. If they are going to be officers they should know what it is like to be closed up at action stations for twelve hours or so at a stretch. That's what would sort out the men from the boys.' He grinned. 'After all, sir, you know the old saying that if there's anything in a boy the sea will bring it out.'

The captain regarded him. 'It's a joke that might have serious results if the general implication of your remarks were carried out,' he said. 'You've got to remember, Harker, that these are soft civilians you've got on your hands. Oh, they've had a few weeks at training depot, but about all that's done for them is to breed a mixture of fear, subservience and suspicion in every mother's son. They aren't sailors then, by a long chalk, although they all think they are, of course, and strut about on leave with their caps flat-a-back and a popsy on each arm. That's when you get them in the *Constant*.' He shifted in his chair and leaned forward on the desk, warming to his theme.

'That kind of potential sea animal is a lot different from a bunch of Dartmouth lads. You and I both know—and you, if you'll forgive me, probably remember better than I—that there is very little in this world tougher than a bunch of R.N. sub-lieutenants out on the razzle. No one plays harder and no one works—and fights—harder and, by God, it's only that that keeps this little island afloat today.' He paused and looked grim.

'Well, most of those chaps are gone, as you know very much better than an old arm-chair sailor like me. They were sacrificed by politicians who thought more of their party line than the country's good and left us without the weapons with which to fight this war. A lot of those boys have been killed in these last months in the Medi, and the flower of the Fleet Air Arm was thrown away in Norway. They leave too many gaps. There aren't nearly enough lads of the same stamp to fill those gaps, so we have to get as near as we can with boys from a very different, a very much softer, more cushioned environment. You can't rub too much salt in *their* backs, Harker. They can't take it. And don't forget—we can't afford to lose them. We need them desperately and we *must* cosset them!'

'That, I think, is precisely the point at issue, sir,' said Harker, 'and if I may say so, I think you are wrong.' He paused, weighing his thoughts.

'Go on,' said the captain keenly.

'Before I was appointed to *Constant*, sir, I should have agreed with you absolutely, and after only a few days on board I should have been more certain than ever.' He uncrossed his legs and leaned forward, resting both hands on the desk top so that the two men, the old and the young, with only one division in rank between them, faced each other, eye to eye, almost as antagonists, partisans of two opposing theories, across the plain of paper-work where the blueprints of action lay thickly scattered.

'Now,' said Harker, 'I would not agree. Since I joined the ship I have grown up, as it were, alongside the class which came on board at the same time as me. I've seen a great deal of them, individually and collectively. They are a terrible cross-bred collection of mongrels, sir. I have schoolmasters—and one or two school*marms*—policemen, shop-walkers, garage mechanics, car salesmen, professional footballers, actors, clerks, stockbrokers and schoolboys—I even have a poet and a dance band crooner. Well, there are a number of weaker brethren in that lot, and they will have to be sorted out at the end of this week—their last week on board—before they waste any more of the righteous tax-payer's money. But I am convinced, sir, that the rest are sound. They've worked hard and tried their best for me. I think they *can* take it!'

'I see,' said the captain. 'You are just as forthright in person as you are on paper, Harker, and of course your opinion will carry great weight with the C.W. Branch—otherwise you would be on the bridge of your own destroyer now, enjoying yourself, instead of going to an old warrior that should have been put out to grass years ago and left there—like me. But I think you must know that your views don't entirely agree with their reports down at *King Alfred*. They say that they are having to pass people as officers down there who are only going to be a damn nuisance in a fighting ship for a long time . . .'

'. . . until they have had their proper experience of sea life in wartime,' broke in Harker. 'And it's precisely that experience, or some of it, that *Constant* should and could be giving them. Otherwise, what is the point of putting them for five weeks in a sea-going ship?'

The captain was silent. He stared at Harker, turning it all over in his mind. The commander took the opportunity to develop his theme even further.

'Oddly enough, sir,' he said, 'it was one of the cadets themselves who, quite unwittingly, put his finger on the trouble.' He paused again, smiling to himself at the recollection of a sulky, blue-jowled young figure on the compass platform. 'He, er, is not a lad I would trust with the *K.G.V,* sir,' he went on. 'In fact he is the poet I mentioned just now that we have in our midst. I had occasion to rap him over the knuckles for failing to do something that was actually totally impossible and I said something to the effect that "This won't do in a ship of war", or something of that sort, and the cheeky young devil pouted and said, "Well, sir, this isn't exactly a ship of war!" Then there was another lad. Nothing wrong with him basically, except for an unfortunate stammer which looked as if it might wash him right out. Four days ago we were off May Island in a real pea-souper and *Implacable* very nearly cut us in two. This lad was his own, and the R.N.V.R.'s, best advocate, because if he hadn't, without the trace of his impediment, given the order which took us clear, that report,' he jabbed a finger towards the typewritten screed which lay on the captain's blotter, 'would not be sitting on your pad, sir, and I would not be here wasting your time!'

The captain looked down at the report and turned over the pages crisply. 'Is that the cadet you mention here?' he asked.

'Yes, sir; Wilsher,' said Harker. 'But the most significant point of the affair came afterwards.' The captain glanced up at him again quickly and raised his eyebrows. 'I asked him,' went on Harker, 'how he managed to get his words out so quickly and clearly—a lad who could hardly answer to his name without falling over his tongue—and he said "I think it was because it was real, sir". That seemed to me to about symbolise what is wrong with the whole scheme at present. It isn't *real*—they feel it and the instructors feel it and the make-believe of it all can't bring out the best in them. Obviously, they can't be given real action, but would it not be priceless to them and to the Navy to create at least the *illusion* of action by turning the *Constant* into a real, sea-going, watchkeeping ship?'

The captain looked at him earnestly for a moment. 'All right,' he said at length, 'what do you propose?'

Harker did not need to be prompted further.

'Cancel the next draft to the ship, sir, and let me take her to sea to cruise, say as far north as Shetland, with the present senior class cadets helping to work the ship—with a bout or two of "action stations" to show them what it's really all about. The idea would be to use this purely as a pilot scheme, if it were successful the idea could be enlarged and made the permanent basis for the training scheme—with classroom and practical instruction being carried out simultaneously, of course, for the remainder of the cadets, plus supplementary instruction in harbour. In that way *Constant*, or, if it were thought expedient to increase the number of ships for training duties, the other ships, would be at sea *all* the time, making the whole scheme one hundred per cent a practical business instead of a half-hearted, chancy affair. Alternatively, a better scheme might well be to use one ship to give preliminary instruction under mild sea-going conditions—the sort of job *Constant* has been doing up to now—and use a second, perhaps newer vessel, to do the actual cruise, with the senior class from the first ship being transferred to her for, say, one week's real sea-time at the end of their, say, four weeks' preliminary instruction, which is the *total* of what they are getting at present. The sea-going ship could carry the senior officer, who would personally interview each cadet on the completion of instruction and sea-time to determine which should be sent on to *King Alfred* and which should be returned "slightly sub-standard".'

The captain made notes. 'You make out a very good case,' he said. 'I shall put it up to the Admiral right away. I think it would be better if you remained in London until a decision has been reached after your scheme has been placed before the Board of Admiralty.'

'Very good, sir,' said Harker, rising to his feet. 'There is just one other thing, sir. Our radar . . .'

'Yes, we've got that in hand,' said the senior officer. 'I'm sorry you've had to wait so long for it, but it won't be much longer. We can't give you one of the latest sets, but you are going to have the one out of the *Rutland*, when she comes in for her refit in a few days' time.'

'I see, sir; thank you, sir,' said the captain of the *Constant*. 'We shall need it badly, particularly if something comes of my idea and we extend our cruise farther north.'

'Quite so,' said the captain. 'Of course in that event we should try to attach you to some Home Fleet force which might be cruising in northern waters—there's always plenty of activity in that area.' He smiled rather grimly. 'Can't have you wandering about on your own with the *Kaiser Wilhelm* making for home waters and God knows what else just waiting in Bergen or Tromso to pick off any of our poor little lambs that stray too far from the fold. Keep that under your hat, by the way.'

Harker's eyes lit up when the name *Kaiser* had been mentioned. Every R.N. captain knew what *Kaiser* stood for and what an anxious time she was giving the Admiralty at this time. When he left Queen Anne's Mansions that morning it was with a strange excitement in his heart.

The captain saw the Rear-Admiral, his superior, that afternoon. Harker never knew, of course, what was said at that meeting or what further ramifications it gave rise to among the hierarchy of the Board of Admiralty, but two days later he found himself on the train staring out of the windows at the ugly suburbs of Grantham again, on his way to rejoin his ship.

In his compartment were two immensely superior second officer Wrens, of the type that considers even Commanders, R.N., very small fry indeed, and half a dozen young Fleet Air Arm pilots and observers. The young men, two of them wearing the purple tabs of midshipmen, R.N.V.R., the others very junior sub-lieutenants, were restless for a little fun but distinctly overawed by the presence of the dark blue duchesses and an elderly commander of thirty-three. Presently they all got up to fight their way to the diner.

As the last of them closed the door behind him the prettier of the two second officers lifted her silly little nose and said,

'The dirty-fingernailed type.'

The other girl, a horsey young woman who was probably an admiral's daughter, answered her with a companionable sneer. Harker looked sharply from one to the other, hating them for snobbish, stupid little bitches from the depths of his soul. With a parting glare he jumped to his feet on impulse and thrust himself out into the crowded corridor in the wake of the young aviators. He was lonely and preferred the society of decent people.

CHAPTER ELEVEN

DICKINSON, in command of *Constant* for three days during the captain's absence in London, had little to do. The senior class was in the midst of its final week aboard and sweating through its written examinations, the rest were grappling with the normal routine of instruction and watchkeeping.

It was a curiously flat and peaceful time. The captain seemed to take with him the sudden flame of violence which had characterised his four weeks of active command. When he went the *Constant* seemed to sigh, loosen her stays and settle down, shrugging off for a spell her role of a fast young lady. Like a young lover, only the captain could make the change in her. The three days became a locked lagoon of peace.

But everyone knew they could not relax completely. The officers were well aware that the captain had gone to the Admiralty to report on his findings after four weeks of the training ship, and half expected sweeping changes of a violent kind in keeping with his nature when he rejoined the ship. The cadets of Nelson division, locked in battle with the Rule of the Road, the anatomy of the simple cell, the stoppages of the Oerlikon gun, doubling the angle on the bow, and all the other science which had been baffling them for four hard weeks now fired at them in a concentrated broadside, were anything but hopeful for the future, facing as they did the examination results and the final dreaded hurdle of the captain's interview.

However, there were no further ugly bursts of arbitrary violence to snarl the smooth course of training; nobody got themselves hurt or went sick.

At last exams were over and the senior cadets could relax a little and indulge themselves by lording it over the greener hands and new arrivals, waiting for the results and the return of the captain.

He was due to return on board on the Friday, and the Nelsons hoped that he would be in time for the concert which they were putting on in the for'ard messdeck that night. This 'end of term' show was a normal weekly feature, put on by the senior class to celebrate their imminent release from the *Constant.*

They had gone to some pains to build up a good show, writing and rehearsing songs and sketches in the dog watches and on make-and-mend afternoons. Wilsher and Moore were the guiding hands in the effort. They each rehearsed a solo spot of their own and appeared in most of the sketches.

The concert began in the evening after rounds. The chief shipwright, who was keenly interested in amateur theatricals, usually constructed the stage and set, which needed very few modifications for each succeeding show, and the senior L.T.O. fixed up a neat row of footlights. He was a little nonplussed to rig the spotlight which Wilsher wanted, and wondered what it could be for. Everybody knew the actor had put himself down for a 'solo' last item on the programme, but no one was any the wiser than that, except that, whatever it was, it must be something out of his repertoire, since it appeared to need no rehearsal.

With great daring they called the show *Mutiny on the Constant.* Cadet rating Rose, who had sung with Ambrose's and Roy Fox's bands before the war, sang several popular songs and a very tall, thin cadet did a clever cross-talk with a very short fat one. A cadet named Lake, who had been a ballet dancer in peacetime executed a clever piece of choreography based upon a rather extraordinary hornpipe which depicted, with some very rude gestures, a typical matelot's run ashore.

Then, in similar vein, Moore came in and sang in an Albert Chevalier cockney to his own small guitar the ballad of *Maggie May,* which all the old timers in the ship's company knew and joined in. Then followed the sketch which gave its name to the show, a skit on *Mutiny on the Bounty,* in which Wilsher, dressed in a borrowed suit of Dickinson's, adjured McCutchen, as Leading Seaman Fletcher Christian, to 'hang all C.W. candidates from the highest yard-arm in the Fleet!'

Moore returned with his guitar and this time gave them a ballad of his own composition. In a light, clear voice he sang his *Sad Harlot Blues*, the little song of the matelot's lady which he had started to compose on lookout duty:

'Sailor, sailor, handsome Jack,
I'll have a gin and knock it back,
Treat me rough like sailors do,
I'm a tramp the same as you.

'Matelot, matelot, you're a dear,
Me with gin and you with beer,
Don't need much of this to make me——
Come on, where you gonna take me?

'Ain't we got no place to go?
Great big stupid so-and-so——
Oh yes, I'll have another, thanks——
No, straight, you're nicer than the Yanks.

'Take me to the churchyard then
When they close at half-past ten,
Roll me over, find me room
In the clover by my tomb.

'In the clover by my tomb. . . .'

With a last, sad note on the refrain, he struck a bitter, jarring chord as he had heard Josh White do in his records and bowed his head. There was silence for a second, then the sudden outburst of loud applause which told him how well his little sad ballad had gone down.

The tone of it exactly set the scene for Wilsher's solo, which immediately followed it. It was only when the young actor opened his mouth to speak the first line that they knew he was going to speak the soliloquy from *Hamlet.*

With a sure flair for theatre and a dash of practical improvisation bodering on genius, Wilsher had decided to do the speech dressed simply in a sailor's bell-bottoms and dark blue jersey. He wore nothing else and went barefoot.

In darkness, except for the L.T.O.'s spotlight playing on him, he began the lines of the greatest poem in the world. . . .

'To be, or not to be, that is the question. . . .'

He played it superbly, with a deep, simple passionate agony of soul which came over, harsh and naked, to every rough matelot and every silly, shallow boy, with such force and conviction that each one felt himself to be witnessing the baring of his soul to the human dilemma of action or acceptance which at different levels racks all mankind. . . .

'Whether 'tis nobler in the mind to suffer
The slings and arrows of outrageous Fortune. . . .'

It was at this point that the captain returned on board. He arrived alongside quickly out of the night, taking the quartermaster and the officer of the day completely by surprise. With a brief salute he walked briskly for'ard.

Ducking into the messdeck entrance, he saw Dickinson glance angrily towards the intrusion, recognise him and start to move towards him. The captain motioned him to silence and joined him quietly at the back of the packed space. He settled down to listen to Wilsher's performance.

'Or to take arms against a sea of troubles,
And by opposing . . . end them. . . .'

The captain leaned across to Dickinson in the darkness.

'My God, this boy is good!' he whispered. 'I'm glad I didn't miss this.'

So the actor went on, intoning the agony of all thinking youth. . . .

'... to die to sleep:
No more; and by a sleep, to say we end
The heart-ache, and the thousand natural shocks
That flesh is heir to? 'tis a consummation
Devoutly to be wished.'

The soliloquy spoke for them all, reading and emptying their eager, anxious minds, as they crouched here, in the for'ard messdeck of H.M.S. *Constant* at Rosyth in the Firth of Forth, on an April evening in the year 1942. For them, for the young, unformed ones, these lines written by an uncouth, brilliant country boy in the sixteenth century, were starkly true. For them, now, the stubborn fight of the will to win through, or the slide to slow ruin in a rotting world.

'To be or not to be,' one of their own number had said, as from his own heart.

Out beyond the shadowy bulk of the ship, down past the other ships and the shore, where the last rays of evening light lay down in the purple shadows of the hills to sleep, out on the darkening sea the wind of tomorrow was already rising.

And deep in the grey Atlantic, far away to the west, a ship called the *Kaiser Wilhelm* steamed towards her destiny.

CHAPTER TWELVE

THE art of the raiding cruiser attained its highest expression in German hands. Its finest flower came early with the brilliance of the famous *Emden*'s depredation's in the Pacific and Indian Oceans. Admiral Graf von Spee, victor at Corónel, beaten and destroyed by battle-cruisers at the Falklands in 1914, was its high priest and patron. His raiders left a trail of smashed ships in their white bubbling wakes. They were the stones flung into a vast blue lake and they set up widening ripples which, like a commercial artist's impression of a bunion, radiated ever wider over our sea-lanes, hardening our vital arteries, slashing at our sea-blue-blooded veins. The ripples reached Whitehall and stung the well-timbered heads of Admirals into such a migraine that they sent Admiral Sturdee with two battle-cruisers to make the buzzing and the pain go away.

By and by it mercifully ceased and Nelson could lie quiet in his tarry silence under the fathoms of the soil once more. Von Spee was dead and his ships, all but the *Dresden, Emden*'s jealous sister, were stones at the bottom of the ocean lake. The escaping cruiser did her worst and did it well, and others followed her. While they flourished they warmed themselves, ate, drank and were as merry as a German can ever genuinely be, on the provender which was supposed to be going to keep the home fires burning in Britain and in the minds of mothers and wives off the terrifying butchery in Flanders.

German expertise dies hard, and when Hitler, the logical and extreme expression of the sensitive, proud, humourless German spirit, started a war to smash his own image in the mirror, the art and science of hitting hard and running fast on enemy trade routes flowered precociously into a neo-freebooting phase. The concept of one fast, dangerous raider loose among the fat sheep of Allied shipping was an inspiration after the self-made supreme megalomaniac's own heart, an inspiration he called his own, a wishful dream, after Wagner, of an Aryan *Flying Dutchman* smashing at the shadows with big noses which sailed arrogantly past his pavement pictures in their golden chariots exhausting jets of cigar smoke.

The lonely ocean raider had his blessing. Out of his ice-cream admiral's suit he pulled his pocket-battleships and sent them to sea, like a sadistic, orphan child launching great fireships in his bath.

But if their origin lay in neurosis, their function was definite and its execution daring and dangerous.

They were there on the great complex of the sea-lanes before the war even began, hooked on the web like spiders. *Deutschland* went out and the *Scheer*, and then the flying ghosts of Spee put to sea from the Fatherland in a ship of that name, under a young, brilliant and ambitious captain named Langsdorff. They fell on our unescorted ships as soon as the bell sounded for the great fight, and threatened to combine their skill and savagery with the U-boats to cut off our supplies and starve us out.

They, and the ships that followed them, went far towards succeeding. At the onset of war it was the surface raiders which the Admiralty most feared, and they made desperate efforts to hunt them down and dispatch them. But this time it wasn't just a matter of sending an Admiral with a powerful fleet especially out from the United Kingdom to deal with a German squadron at the other side of the world, like a king to checkmate a king. This time the raiders were scattered like solitary, spiteful wolves all over the oceans of the world. And there was no Grand Fleet this time, no huge glut of dreadnoughts which would not miss two battle-cruisers and half a squadron of cruisers. This time we were desperately short of all kinds of warships and especially of cruisers.

But by slow and painful degrees it was managed. When the European war allowed, ships were gathered in ones and twos from all over the key points of the ocean fronts and arranged in a giant complex of hunter-killers to smell out and sink the raiders. By the brilliance and tenacity of individual commanders and the dogged thoroughness of the search, they brought the wolves one by one into a corner. One or two escaped, although with such a fright that they were never sent out again, the remainder were caught and scotched.

Symbol of this victory was the end of the *Graf Spee*. She was trapped by the genius of Commodore Harwood in the confines of the Plate, and for her there could be no escape. Even if she succeeded, cruelly battered as she was, in smashing through the guard of cruisers that ringed the mouth of the great river, she could never hope to evade the wide-ranging eyes of the pilots from the carrier *Ark Royal,* steaming flat-out from Rio towards her. It was the aircraft carrier, in fact, the new Queen of the Seas, which put the raiding cruiser finally out of business.

Langsdorff, a tragic, beaten figure, asked his patron for guidance. The inmate of Berchtesgaden, his shadows suddenly become reality, told him to give in, Langsdorff put the match to his beautiful ship, then a gun to his own head and scattered his glorious, Aryan dream forever.

After *Spee,* the art slowly died. Warships put to sea and worked the Atlantic but their efforts were half-hearted and when the mighty *Bismark,* then the *Scharnhorst,* were sunk the whole idea collapsed and no German commander gave ocean raiding a serious thought again. After that they were content to talk from their arm-chairs of the passive power of their 'fleet in being' and allow comfortable constipation to atrophy their will to attack as they filled the wardroom of the harbour-bound *Tirpitz* with their ersatz fighting talk.

All, that is, except Kapitan Helmuth König. König was the youngest captain on the Nazi Navy list. He had been junior even to Langsdorff and had ideas of his own about what the dead captain should have done when he faced despair in Montevideo. Kapitan König considered that Langsdorff had made too many mistakes, mistakes which had lost him many a fat British merchantman and which had culminated in the blunder of underestimating a British commodore. The blunder, thought König grimly, had cost the Reich a pocket battleship, and had been staggeringly costly at the price. If he had had the *Spee*. . . .

König, full of theories and fired by supreme confidence in his own abilities, longed for a ship, a powerful, hard-hitting fighting ship, with which to put his theories into practice. For he had one very special idea which he thought he might be able to sell to Raeder or, better still, anybody who had the Fuehrer's ear. . . .

But there *was* nobody, and, even if there had been, commands of any kind in the German Navy nowadays were scarcer than British victories and there were many names above his on the list of seniority. Then, one evening at a rather drunken party in the Navy headquarters in Berlin, luck befell him. König was the only one at the party who was not drunk. He wasn't even hazy. He was never hazy. He sat now, his back against the blackout curtain, staring in front of him. There was a glass at his elbow but the glass contained water, by arrangement between himself and the barman, an old rating who had been his servant in the *Deutschland.* König was never hazy, always cold sober, always ice-clear, always thinking—and it was always the main chance that occupied his thoughts. His thoughts cut and probed at his big problem at this moment like an old sailor's cutlass slashing away the wreckage of a shattered mast which stopped his swift passage through the water. But this time the tangle was tough and it was beginning to blunt that sharp, swinging blade. . . . Why had he never joined The Party? Why had he preferred the hard way of sheer duty and daring and brilliance when a few meaningless words might long ago have given him the *Hipper* or the *Eugen*, even the *Spee*? . . .

He thought back, imagining himself as he had been, ruthlessly laying bare the soul of Leutnant König. He had been a simple sailor then, he decided, a *very* simple sailor, too quick to scorn the landbound brown jobs that ran the Reich, his eyes too glazed by staring over the ocean distances, his tongue too bitter with its salt. . . . König was a good sailor, a real sailor, and in his heart he had the disgust and suspicion for the bullies and perverts he saw in high office every day which any deep-sea man the world over would have felt. But he was too much of a sailor ever to be able to do without the sea, without the swaying deck of a ship and the thirst of the wide, green seas. He did not know any other way of getting what he wanted than in the jostling, crowded wardrooms of the German Navy. And he was ambitious, more desperately so because his ambition was fed, not by neurotic dreams and chimeras like so many German officers, but by a clear, sure knowledge of his real greatness as a seaman.

It seemed he was not ambitious enough. Otherwise—why had he not joined The Party and bought his passport to immortality? What did it really matter that he had called the price of this so often 'seventeen pieces of silver'? Who was he to change the way things were?

He sat there on the fringe of the party, on the edge of the world, the only world he knew, on the outside looking in, his eyes as icy-blue as the Baltic, a blond, square-faced, sturdy young man, fingering the long white scar where a splinter of steel from one of Warburton-Lee's destroyers at Narvik had left a white wake down his temple. Command? The only thing he would ever command was the desk he sailed at Kiel, giving orders to the fräulein typists, most of them perpetually pregnant by some big-arsed Luftwaffe pilot or one of those revolting vermin in black.... Bitter with self-pity, he sat and stared, a raider without a thing to raid, a wolf without any sheep, and a lone wolf into the bargain....

Then, hull-down but sweet and fast and making smoke, a fat prize steamed across his anxious, mid-ocean search. She was a well-shaped, expensive, lovely lady, a luxury yacht such as you seldom saw in the Reich these days. She was not a fräulein typist and she was not pregnant by a Luftwaffe glamour boy. If she was pregnant by anybody, it would be Herr Goebbels. For Fräulien Hilda Geissler, besides adorning the Berlin stage, also—and this was of vital significance to Helmuth König in his present state of acute frustration—was known all over the Reich to be the little club-footed neurotic's latest mistress.... König's blue eyes shone with the lust of battle. He raised his sights, rang down for maximum revolutions and cleared away for action. With his glass of water gripped firmly in his brown seaman's hand he set course for Fräulein Hilda.

It took a long time, and it was a dangerous, uncharted passage, made perilous by sudden broadsides of guilty passion and trembling, stealthy soundings. But in the end he reached harbour. He sat in the captain's quarters of the pocket battleship *Kaiser Wilhelm,* steam on all her boilers and orders after his own heart in the envelope under his hand. Upon him were the hopes of the Reich and the German Navy, behind him the promise of the biggest propaganda campaign an officer of the Reich had ever had since Francke—and the broken heart of Fräulein Geissler.

The great wave of optimism which accompanied the invasion of Russia in June 1941, helped the young captain to his command. With the rapid initial success of the blitzkrieg on land came the resurgence of a feeling in high naval circles that perhaps, after all, the time was ripe for further sorties by those heavy warships which remained serviceable. *Eugen* was available, though *Scharnhorst* and *Gneisenau* were damaged and would not be serviceable for some months to come. *Bismarck* had gone, but her mighty sister was almost ready to go to sea. *Kaiser,* new and untried, was ready to lead the spearhead of the new offensive at sea.

König was given the *Kaiser* in the summer of 1941. All that summer and autumn she worked up. König was by training a gunnery specialist, and he saw to it that his ship was the finest gunnery ship in a navy always renowned for its superlative marksmanship. When autumn came he was confident that he had a superb ship and a ship's company that was the finest in the world, and he looked forward to his sailing orders.

He received them in late November, on the very day, symbolically enough, when his newly acquired patron Goebbels announced that a U-boat had sunk the proud British carrier *Ark Royal.* König hoped that this time the news was true. The carrier, a sharp thorn in the flesh of the Axis for so long now, almost the symbol of the dogged British resistance at sea, had been 'sunk' many times, but only by the paper bombs of the propaganda ministry. He hoped, too, that the friendship and favour of the little poison merchant would not rebound upon him as it had upon the head of the unfortunate Francke, the

Luftwaffe pilot whom Goebbels had puffed into the hero of the first 'sinking' of the *Ark Royal,* and who was subsequently discredited, ruined and brought to the verge of suicide.

The sinking at last of the ship which had brought about the loss of the *Bismarck* came when the fortunes of the Royal Navy were at a low ebb, when she was struggling to recover from grievous losses sustained in the Atlantic and Mediterranean. At the same time it was the gloomy herald of even worse disasters to come. *Bismarck,* though gone, had taken the high and mighty *Hood* with her and severely mauled the brand new *Duke of York,* pride of the British Fleet. In the Mediterranean the Luftwaffe had decimated Admiral Cunningham's ships, sinking many of his priceless cruisers and destroyers and driving the seriously damaged carriers *Illustrious* and *Formidable* out of the Italian Lake altogether to seek rest and repair in American yards. The Royal Navy was left with a handful of battleships, cruisers and destroyers, and in carriers reduced to the perilous strength of one new ship, the *Victorious* and three old, worn-out veterans with a few obsolete aircraft between them. Across the troubled, perilous Atlantic, which Allied convoys crossed bravely in the teeth of a mounting U-boat offensive, the United States seemed apathetic and isolationist, in spite of her Lend-Lease agreement with Britain, and in any case her fleet was idle, unpractised and unprepared.

Such was the state of civilization's police force when yet another dangerous, deadly criminal broke loose and began to run amok among its sorely hurt peoples.

Kaiser had just weighed and was heading for the boom when König received, by visual signal from the tower, the news that Japan had crashed into the war by destroying the American Fleet at Pearl Harbour. He felt a pang of professional jealousy at the news, both for himself and for the Navy he served which, so proud in tradition and in skill, was yet so poor in numbers compared with the upstart Japanese barbarians. The bitter feelings stiffened his resolve and sharpened his ambition even further. He realised of course, that an ally is always to be welcomed, albeit with caution, and the great power of the Japanese Fleet and Army would drive the Allies, already badly hit, to the very extremes of their resources of manpower, material and courage. Now Rommel would smash through the Middle East and join hands with the Japanese Army in India. Now the Navy of Nippon, strong in carriers and immense new battleships, would sweep first the Pacific, then the Indian Ocean, and, when the Royal Navy was almost annihilated, the German Fleet would thrust north about from its harbours, and down the great ocean which the U-boats would by then have turned into a German Lake, to meet the massed ships of Yamamoto at the place where the *Spee* had taken with her those early hopes of victory for the Swastika at sea. What would happen when German and Japanese met as joint conquerors of the world, of course, when giant *Tirpitz* came close aboard giant *Yamato,* was another matter, and only the cynics gave it thought.

This was the vision of Helmuth König, this was the future he painted in glowing terms to his officers on the newly painted bridge of *Kaiser,* as she crept north from Germany, trusting to her new radar—better than anything the British had—and to the long nights and bad weather of the coming winter to hide her and keep her from her watchful enemies until she could reach the place where her guns would speak for the first time.

Only König knew where that was. Following the winking message from the signal tower had come a fast motor launch with new and secret orders for the captain of the *Kaiser,* orders which, modified at the eleventh hour by Nagumo's world shaking blow, amplified and extended his original brief in a way which gladdened his heart and made his blue, Baltic eyes glitter with a zealot's fire. . . .

CHAPTER THIRTEEN

KÖNIG reached the North Cape, northernmost point of Europe, unseen and unmolested, having crept quietly by night up the Leads, the narrow tongue of water which separates the rocky coast of Norway from her outer bastion of islands. It was a feat of considerable achievement, demanding great nerve and superb seamanship. Helmuth König had these things in abundance and so had his band of picked officers.

From there it was comparatively easy to pass through the wild wastes of the Denmark Strait between Iceland and Greenland. He did it in the worst weather for many years, when no aircraft could live in the air above the ocean and no surface ship could have engaged him even if they had sighted him. In fact there were no ships on patrol. The Royal Navy had no cruiser available in this terrible hour and had abandoned using armed merchant cruisers ever since the martyrdom of the *Jervis Bay*—sunk by *Kaiser's* consort *Scheer*.

He was not seen, and when he broke into the Atlantic he used his very powerful new radar so skilfully that he was able absolutely to avoid contact with even the shadow of any of the many ships his operators saw on their screens, fast, unescorted ships or slow, lumbering convoys alike.

Of course he had to suppress firmly the desire to forget the calculating brain of his radar and rush in among these helpless lambs. He would make a glorious killing while he lasted, but he would not last very long.... That was the mistake the others had made. He was König—König of the *Kaiser*. That was how he thought of himself already, that was how all Germany and the world would soon know him—if he could keep cool and function with the precision and infallibility of that little concave shield revolving at the masthead, endlessly probing with the unseen antenna of which König, red-eyed and alert, could see only the reflection in green kinks on the unwinking orange eye of the repeater.

These kinks were Allied ships. Some of them wondered why the U-boats were not so active this trip. Most of them put it down, fairly enough, to the atrocious weather. That was quite enough, thank you. To some extent they were right, of course, but had they known the main reason for their immunity they would have fought the Admiralty weather with a less clear and single-minded resolve.

For the U-boats, strung out in single units and in packs right across the convoy lanes, had been mobilised to give *Kaiser* a helping hand. From their detailed and intimate knowledge of British movements they were able to pass her, as it were, from hand to hand, König using them as stepping stones and with as little regard for his weary and unshaven submarine colleagues as if they had been doormats. They, in their turn, resented this thankless chore which threw their calculated, hard-won chances of success out of gear. More than one tired and dirty Leutnant-zur-See cursed the youngest captain on the German Navy list as he watched fat targets pass in gormless parade across his periscope eye, targets he was forbidden to engage lest the commotion brought warships to the area and jeopardised *Kaiser*'s chances of a clean break-through. More than one watched his big consort out of periscope range, slanging the dashing raider captain who would get all the glory while they waited in the darkness of green fathoms in their steel coffins for the thankless victory of another British tanker sent to the bottom and, at the end, a ghastly death by drowning or choking by chlorine gas. But König's imagination did not stretch deep enough to feel their frustration and jealousy. He merely walked on them to glory.

At last he was free of the greatest danger, heading south with his faithful supply ship through the blue and gold welcome of the South Atlantic. He was in his proper country now, the wide acres of blue ocean ploughed by the *Emden* and the heels of Spee's old squadron, by the ship *Spee* and by all the great raiders who had gone before him. He was the latest of them and he would be the greatest of all. He would be König of the *Kaiser*.

His nearest brush with disaster came when *Kaiser* narrowly missed contact with a British carrier intended in fact for Admiral Phillips' force at Singapore which was preparing to attack the Japanese, but delayed on working-up practice in the West Indies by damage. The new carrier was a fast ship and a slack radar operator allowed her to come almost within range of the British ship's less powerful set before he made his report. After a patrolling aircraft from the same ship almost spotted the pocket battleship, all König could do was to hold his breath and curse. But the plane did not appear within visual range and they went on their way unmolested.

König was naturally annoyed that his ship could do nothing to hurt the British carrier. But he did what he could by proxy. He relayed the enemy's position to a nearby U-boat pack. Six hours later the U-boats sank her. Admiral Phillips did not get his air cover and later suffered grievously for lack of it.

König gave the port of Freetown, in Sierra Leone, a wide berth, fearing that there might be strong British forces in harbour there but at last, when he was 100 miles south of it, he broke the new ship's virgin record by sinking a merchantman.

He sank two more on the following day, before he left the area and headed west on the first leg of a triumphant zig-zag progress down the South Atlantic. At the end of this greedy tour he had sunk twelve ships. He could have sunk many more, simply by turning and retracing his steps, but it was too great a risk. Langsdorff had overreached himself in just such a way when he had made that last fatal cocksure lunge at the rich traffic of the Plate. This was not Langsdorff. This was König of the *Kaiser*.

Kaiser herself went well clear of that area. She must have been reported by now, however vaguely, and British warships might even now be chasing her from the north. If they were, they were in for a long run, for he had no intention of staying in the South Atlantic, let alone turn north into their jaws.

But he made one glorious, intensely satisfying geasture before departing thence. Intelligence had told him that there were no longer any British ships based at Port Stanley in the Falkland Islands. So König went and threw a few shells into the harbour where Von Spee had seen the tripod masts of Sturdee's battle cruisers and read his doom there. Every eleven-inch shell which left *Kaiser*'s for'ard turret was one for Spee and for Hans Langsdorff. In case he should be observed, König hoisted Japanese colours. Let them work *that* one out, he mused. Then he vanished like a bushwhacker into the hazy blue horizon, leaving only a wispy pennant of smoke rising like an Indian signal.

König was heading for a place where the British Navy was very weak—the Indian Ocean. This had always been a favourite hunting ground for German raiders. He entered it by a roundabout but profitable route, sinking three ships in the Mozambique Channel and two more off the Maldive Islands. He knew he was safe. Britain had only one big carrier operating and it was obvious that she would save that one for her home defence. As for cruisers—they were all at Singapore, what there was left of them, or in the Dutch East Indies, fighting desperately to slow down the swiftly advancing Japanese. König, besides being an able and daring man, was a very lucky one, for he had left Germany on the crest of a wave, when the Allied effort at sea was about to be stretched almost too thin to hold—when the punctures made by an ocean raider would be felt more than ever before.

He went on with his depredations, sinking ships wherever he found them. The Royal Navy could not spare a single ship to stop him, for, by the closing days of February, 1942, the cruel battle of the Java Sea had begun.

It was the last stand of the Allied navies in the East. We had already suffered many savage losses to our naval strength. Admiral Phillips, waiting at Singapore for the air support which never came—thanks to König and the U-boats—at last could delay no longer. He sailed to fight the Japanese with the battle-cruiser *Repulse* and the new battleship *Prince of Wales*, and was never seen again. Japanese heavy bombers had obliterated him. König's chances of glory, already borne aloft on Hokusai's surging wave, rose even higher. He began to attack isolated, unescorted warships—if they were small enough—and sank two sloops, an old destroyer and an armed merchant cruiser.

It was then that rumours of a great battle reached him, rumours of a battle now being fought behind that long green curtain of islands which, curving down from Singapore to New Guinea, hid the great lagoon of the Java Sea from the vast, trackless stretch of sea where *Kaiser,* temporarily skulking in the long grass, lay watching for prey.

The cupboard, however, was bare for the present and the scent of a great battle made König's mouth water. Here was a glorious chance for German arms to lead the van in the East, a chance to show the imitative Japanese how to fight a modern engagement at sea. He headed *Kaiser* for Java.

He arrived rather late for the fat pickings he had imagined. When *Kaiser* entered the Sunda Straits the main slaughter was over. A scratch force of British, American and Dutch cruisers and destroyers had been almost annihilated by overwhelming Japanese might, both on the sea and in the air, and by now only the broken remnants which had somehow escaped the fury were left. These ships, like wounded animals, were dotted over that pitiless, steel-polished sea, limping and almost dead with pain and weariness, fighting desperately to reach one of the gaps in the outer bastion of islands, normally smiling in the sun, now frowning like great prison walls, which would be their door to rest and freedom and life. But few of them ever reached it.

As *Kaiser* left the Straits and poked her heavy Germanic bows into the Java Sea, her radar picked up a ship ahead. The green kick of her echo on the pocket battleship's radar was large. A few minutes' careful searching and plotting by the leading operator soon established that the other ship was following a parallel course to their own—heading in the opposite direction, trying to get through the door which had let the German in. The two ships, as far as König could accurately estimate, were practically bow to bow, on a collision course. She was slightly smaller than *Kaiser,* and she was moving very, very slowly. The German radar operator guessed a cruiser and König was inclined to agree. *Kaiser* cleared away for action.

Twenty minutes later her masthead lookout raised a tiny feather of smoke on the horizon, bearing about 010 degrees on the starboard bow.

Five minutes went by and the lookout raised the shout,

'British cruiser!'

König and all the officers on the bridge kept their glasses levelled on the black smudge ahead. A mast appeared, then a control top, then the top part of a bridge.

It was the bridge which gave her away instantly to König. Had he not pored for hours, as soon as the first news of *Spee*'s last fight had come through, over the silhouettes and salient features of all the ships Langsdorff might expect to have to engage, fighting the battle for him, weighing the *Spee*'s chances against each and against any given combination of those ships; weighing, too, Harwood's prospects of damaging the heavier pocket-battleship?

That bridge? He would know it anywhere. It was the *Taunton*. In a matter of minutes his eleven-inch guns were firing on her. In a few more minutes the sadly battered veteran was on fire from stem to stern. In half an hour from the moment of first sighting she was gone and König was picking up survivors. There were not many of them, and most of these had already been grievously wounded by Japanese bombs and shells. The captain of the *Kaiser* was exhilarated. He had avenged the *Spee*. He had wiped out that disgrace.

Just as the last of *Kaiser*'s boats had reached the davit head once more, planes appeared on the horizon. They were Japanese torpedo bombers and they were after the *Taunton*.

The leader of the formation was very young and he and his fellow pilots were filled with the wild *banzai* of attack. They had been told to find, fix and strike a warship in a certain position. When they reached that position they found a warship there and they attacked her. She flew no colours and was fair game. The Japanese squadron commander had no knowledge of any German raider in the area. How could he, since König had taken this move on his own initiative, and, in any case, liaison between the two navies was as yet almost non-existent?

What these bombers tried to do on this day did nothing to

expedite the union.

König saw instantly the ghastly mistake of the Japanese leader. He did what he could, turning *Kaiser* in immediate avoiding action, having the cool presence of mind to pass the order to his gunners above all, no matter what the provocation, not to fire upon the planes of their Allies. The result of a pitched battle between the navies of Germany and Japan at this stage in the war was too awful to think of.

The leader came in and dropped his torpedo, then the next plane and the next. König combed their tracks with consummate skill. By now the biggest German ensign in her signal locker was whipping angrily from *Kaiser*'s truck.

But it was too late to stop the fourth torpedo. The dark blue lethal thing struck the pocket battleship right aft.

Her rudder was instantly blown into a twisted, distorted shape. She began to career in wild circles all round the Java Sea. Then, and only then, did the horrified Japanese leader see what he had done, and call off the attack.

König, on his bridge, had more common sense than to jump and rave and tear his hair. He knew full well that part of the blame was his for playing a lone German hand in a Japanese parish. He contented himself with righting the material wrong and taking the necessary steps to bring his ship under command and to make way again through the water.

CHAPTER FOURTEEN

Kaiser spent six weeks in Singapore, which had fallen to the Japanese, after this outrage of mistaken identity. Neither side made any outcry and the affair was of necessity hushed up. At Singapore the ambitious German captain watched the swift flood of Japanese conquest sweep over the whole of the vast Eastern Archipelago, from Sumatra, 3,000 miles east to the Solomons. He saw one half of his vision of an Axis conquest coming true. The Japanese threw their army into Burma to threaten India, and their naval forces at New Guinea and the Solomons—a giant, two-fisted grab designed to envelop half the world. König looked in vain to the west for signs of a parallel German thrust eastwards. But westward land and sea were dark. Rommel beat in vain on the gates of Egypt and the Allied navies still held the great channel of the Atlantic.

When would the great German naval sortie come? König, dock-bound in Singapore, fretted. Now was the time to strike; now, when British naval strength was at its lowest ebb and America still so groggy from the Pearl Harbour attack that the Japanese could send a big fleet to Singapore, when the U-boats in the Atlantic were mounting a murderous offensive, when *Scharnhorst* and *Gneisenau*—recently escaped from Brest—*Kaiser* and *Scheer* and *Lutzow* and the mighty *Tirpitz* herself, were all ready to lead the German Fleet to a glorious victory which would wipe out forever the shame of 1918.

König, impatient, ambitious, sent dispatch after dispatch back to the Reich from Singapore and a flood of private messages to Herr Goebbels advocating in impassioned tones this grand vision he had.

He did not argue in vain. Already the Propaganda Ministry had built up the name of König of the *Kaiser* to heroic status.

His daring and successful ocean raids had come at a time when Germany badly needed news of a famous victory. The army was bogged down in Russia and Rommel stalemated in Africa. Then the star of König of the *Kaiser* rose in the east and German morale soared Valhalla-wards on his tail.

The legends grew about his name and glory. Bit by bit the propaganda snowball rolled on, faster and ever faster. His name now eclipsed Rommel's and was the darling of the Fuehrer's lips. 'As the American Lincoln once said of his General Grant, "I cannot spare this man—he fights," ' the great man was heard to say.

Soon the golden dream, dreamed first to König himself, planted in the German consciousness by Goebbels and watered by the tears of Nazi frustration, of a great sortie of German naval might at sea began to hum in the electric air of Berlin and Berchtesgaden. The time was ripe and overripe for such a move. The U-boats were winning in the west, the little Japs were smashing the remaining puny Allied warships in the east. 'Strike at sea—strike NOW!' became the parroted slogan. Allied agents caught the scent of the prevailing wind, though there was little enough the Royal Navy could do about it by way of preparation. The Japanese High Command, too, were informed of this new wave of interest in the German Navy. They knew well enough, too, that the man whose white-hot ambition had inspired it lay fretting in his impotence in their new dockyard at Singapore as a result of bungling by their own men.

The dream marched on and by and by became a recommendation, then a proposal, finally a plan. The great sortie was on. All it needed was a leader.

There could be but one choice. He must return at once from the east and bring his ship with him. Pressure waves flowed from Berlin to Tokyo. As an immediate result the repairs to *Kaiser* received top priority. König, his destiny manifest at last in all its brassy glory, made ready to take his brave ship back to the Fatherland through the very heart of its enemies. It was a task fraught with greatest danger, but like that great wily sailor Odysseus, he knew his own craft and strength and cunning and was resolved he could win through—he must. The future of the

Fatherland depended upon him. The Wehmacht, the stupid brown jobs; the perverts of the Gestapo; the glamorous Luftwaffe—all had failed her, but the German Navy, with König of the *Kaiser* to lead it, would not fail her.

By way of a goodwill gesture and to screen the real aim of his departure from Singapore, König was loaned to the Japanese for a spell.

With no serious opposition to fear at present from the United States Navy, the Japanese had been able to bring heavy naval forces to the Indian Ocean. Now they commanded this sea and Britain had neither the ships nor the aircraft to dispute its possession.

She had a tiny 'fleet in being', which she was pleased to call her 'Eastern Fleet'—a title which made even the poker-faced Admiral Nagumo at Singapore smile—consisting of three old battleships, a few cruisers and destroyers and the little old carrier *Hermes,* but so complete was Japanese domination of the Indian Ocean that this feeble squadron dared not go as far east as Ceylon, the eastern-most harbour still in British hands. It had its being at Addu Atoll in the Maldive Islands, 450 miles further west. The British Admiral there could never hope to control events in the Bay of Bengal. All he could do was to hope that such puny strength as he had might interfere with Japanese attempts to attack the routes to western India. It was König's hope that he might at least be allowed to attack these routes now with *Kaiser,* but at the time he could not guess that Germany had selected him for a greater destiny.

It was unlikely, he thought, that the British forces could hope to stop the great strength which Nagumo had collected at Singapore. On April Fool's Day he counted four battleships, five aircraft carriers and a large array of cruisers and destroyers anchored in the harbour.

On 3rd April their fleet sailed west. With it went the rejuvenated *Kaiser* in an honoured position in the van. Their objective was Ceylon. If they could capture it, then the Japanese would be in Alexandria in plenty of time to open the front door for Rommel. Even if they only smashed some of the British warships on the way there and drew to Ceylon forces the Allies badly needed elsewhere, not to mention the blow this would deal to British prestige in India, the attack would be counted a glorious success.

On the 5th, Nagumo's carrier planes struck Colombo and sank a cruiser and a destroyer. But for a number of Royal Air Force Hurricanes they would have sunk many more ships. Next day, however, they sank two eight-inch cruisers at sea, and during the next few days the Axis forces sank or captured a hundred thousand tons of shipping in the Bay of Bengal, a large share of this priceless spoil falling to the matchless gunnery of König's men. On the 9th they attacked Ceylon again and sank the *Hermes* with all her aircraft. A gallant desperate attack was made upon the Japanese Fleet by Royal Air Force Blenheims but these were all shot down—one by the *Kaiser*, which was her first aircraft victory.

After this Nagumo turned east again and made for Singapore. As he did so he made inscrutable and polite signals to his brilliant colleague Kapitan König, who was for the grey Atlantic and a dangerous passage home. The Japanese admiral knew that all the Axis navies had achieved so far was as nothing compared with the battles they must fight when Britain and America found their strength, watched the proud peacock plume of smoke from *Kaiser*'s funnel and wished the young zealot luck with the howling pack that he would somehow have to out-run in the North Atlantic and the frozen Arctic seas.

Kaiser and König vanished utterly and were not seen or heard from again for many long days. Only the seagulls saw her at the very extreme of their sorties from land, only the winds of mid-ocean spoke her. Through the whole of the South Atlantic she ploughed her lonely white furrow and grew more green herself with barnacle and bitter salt as she sailed. First it was cruising stations, then red-eyed watch-and-watch for the ship's company, then perpetual nightmare action stations, as she threaded with infinite caution the criss-crossed convoy lanes of the North Atlantic.

Now the U-boat captains cursed her again, for now, with the uneasy threat of a pocket battleship once more loose somewhere at sea, the British scraped the barrel for convoy escorts and made their vital job more difficult. But they knew how equally vital was the safe passage of this salt-encrusted ship, for when they looked through their periscopes now at the *Kaiser* they knew they were watching a future Admiral of the High Seas Fleet sailing to glory.

Sub-Lieutenant Derek Hewitt-Johnson had ridden to hounds ever since he could remember. He was blooded at the age of seven by his tough old admiral father, and later found another outlet for his ebullient spirit by racing very fast cars at Brooklands and all over the Continent. When war broke out he had made himself, with the easy, lazy effort of the natural athlete, an expert private pilot as well. On 3rd September 1939, therefore, it was not surprising to find a languid young man seeking an interview at the Admiralty.

'I've got an aeroplane,' he said to a surprised and amused senior officer. 'Would you like it?'

The Navy took the gift horse and its jockey as well. And now here he was, cheerfully settled in among a wardroom of seasoned, salted professional seamen, half-way across the Atlantic from Halifax. The Merchant Navy officers were on the alert, expecting trouble. Derek Hewitt-Johnson was also on the alert, looking forward to some.

Unter-Leutnant Hans Froebal, on the other hand, was not looking forward to it. He was an intense young man and would have made a good Nazi officer if only he could have been intense about flying instead of music. For Froebal had been launched into the Party much more by the Aryan purity of Wagner than by the virgin call of arms.

The wild seascape below him now was a tone poem to Hans Froebal, a poem made the more sombre and significant by the long, lean wolfish shape threading the counterpoint of the waves with the bright needle of a bow-wave and the brassy bravado of her flaunting ensign. He had been told to keep a lookout for the *Kaiser* and help her if need be.

As it so happened Froebal could help her, or thought he could. He had left his station over the British convoy to confirm that the grey shadow on the horizon to the south was indeed the

German vessel. He found her, circled her and flashed her the information that a British convoy lay to the north-east of him. On her present course, Froebal estimated roughly, the pocket battleship would clear the tail-end ships of the convoy but might come within radar range of them. The British were getting much improved radar these days and you never knew. . . .

König damned the pilot's good offices. His own radar had already told him as much and he was on the point of giving the wheel order which would put him out of danger.

Leutnant Froebal had meant well, but it would have been better for himself, the *Kaiser* and the Reich if he had stayed at his post with the convoy instead of giving it a vague and cursory check-up then making off with a phrase of *The Flying Dutchman* on his lips towards the flying German who did not need his clumsy assistance.

For then he might have noticed the catapult ship at the stern end of the convoy. But he did not notice her. Derek Hewitt-Johnson had sharper eyes and a much more single mind and he saw the sinister, prowling shape of the Focke-Wulf as she nosed from one cloud patch to another.

As he felt the kick in the arse which shot the Hurricane off the catapult and over the blunt bows he felt a great surge of heart. It was like fox-hunting, only better and more real. Besides, he was glad to leave the ship, comfortable as she was. It *had* been a bit embarrassing telling chaps that you were in a ship called the *Empire Banana.*

Froebal did not see him until it was very much too late. He saw him, in fact, with dying eyes, just before the control column slipped from his hands and the plane dived into the sea off *Kaiser*'s bows, both the pilots dead.

The Hurricane had appeared out of a cloud and fired one short burst to finish off the snooper. König had had the helpless Focke-Wulf in his sights as well, and fired off a burst of sailor's language just as Hewitt-Johnson pressed his firing button. Then, as he saw the Kondor fall, the German captain gave the order to open fire.

As the Hurricane flew straight and level along *Kaiser*'s starboard side trying to keep below her arc of fire, he was hit by a spray of cannon shell and blew up in a flaming ball. Derek Hewitt-Johnson had made his last and finest view.

Before he fell, however, he had managed to do what König feared he might do. He had reported the presence of the *Kaiser*. In actual fact he got no farther than the words 'Pocket battleship . . .' before he died, but the convoy picked up these laconic words and passed them to H.Q. Western Approaches at Liverpool.

The pocket battleship, when sighted by the observer in a Swordfish, was in a position 53° 35 N, 10° 40 W, steering 075^{b}.

By this course she was heading straight for Fair Isle.

König, guessing as soon as he sighted the single Swordfish shadowing him that heavy forces must be lying in wait to the north of him, had made a bold and brilliant decision—to cut east between Shetland and the Orkneys and trust that there were insufficient forces in that area to stop him. It was a gamble, but it was a superbly intelligent one.

The Swordfish contained two gallant but over-enthusiastic officers. Knowing how vital it was that the German should be stopped and believing him to be in a position in which he could be easily shadowed by shore-based aircraft, they made a lone attack on her with bombs to try to inflict enough damage to slow her down.

Coming in high, they made a dive-bombing attack on the *Kaiser*. Roaring down in an almost vertical dive, for which the old aircraft they flew had never been designed, they released their bombs and pulled out of their dive so low that the telegraphist air-gunner was able to swing his gun round and shatter the windows of her bridge. Then the guns of the pocket battleship silenced him and shot the brave Stringbag to pieces. König, straightening up after ducking to avoid the spray of bullets, had to suppress the impulse to salute the blob of blazing wreckage as *Kaiser*'s bow-wave drenched the oily flame with white spray.

Ashore, more and more men and women in naval headquarters and stations were being mobilised to form vital parts in the great complex being swiftly and frantically built to trap the raider.

At first only the Admiral, Western Approaches, was concerned and the Commander-in-Chief, Home Fleet. Then, when news came that *Kaiser* was heading by a short cut for the North Sea, every naval station north of the Humber was brought into the picture. They knew she was the *Kaiser* now—that much had been easy as soon as she had been identified as a pocket battleship. The realisation immediately made the hunt doubly urgent. This was no ordinary raider they were after. This was König. Every sea officer in the Navy, and most of the British public too, now knew of the brilliant buccaneering ocean raider who was greater than the pirates of old. Like Rommel's on land, König's was indeed a name to conjure with, and secretly fear, on the sea. Naval Intelligence, closely informed of the state of affairs in German naval circles, knew the greater importance of this young captain. They knew he was coming home to lead the Navy of the Fatherland in a great onslaught at sea, perhaps to rise even higher and lead a fumbling, faltering state. The Scipio who had saved Rome was a mere lad of thirty-two ... König must be stopped.

At headquarters they all knew this. The Admiral knew it, standing grave and grim among his staff, facing the great wall map of the northern seas.

The Air Staff Officer on the Admiral's staff knew it, and knew that he had no aircraft to send after the flying raider. *Implacable,* the only carrier in northern waters, was speeding southwards with her squadron, but *Kaiser* was still many miles out of striking range of her aircraft. There were no strike aircraft at Kirkwall, in the Orkneys; only fighters, and none at any of the other Naval air stations in Northern Command.

Then he remembered the half-formed R.A.F. Beaufort squadron at Wick.... There might be a chance....

'Sir!'

'Yes?' The Admiral swung round swiftly.

'Sir, the Beauforts at Wick, sir. They're a new squadron, just forming. They might....'

'Get me the A.O.C. at once,' said the Admiral.

'Sir!' The timid voice of the Wren at his elbow made itself

heard over the chatter and clatter of telephones.

'Well?'

'Sir, there's a message from Admiralty. Training cruiser *Constant* at present steering 185 degrees one hundred miles east-nor-east of Fair Isle, sir. They are unable to contact her and they're worried about her present position in relation to the enemy.'

The Admiral looked swiftly at the map. The Wren in slacks at the top of the ladder had already indicated the last known position, course and speed of *Constant* with a flag and arrow.

The Admiral stared blankly at the arrow. His eyes went across to the black arrow marking *Kaiser*'s course from the west.

There was a moment of silence in the room, a feak of quiet like a vacuum in nature.

'If she continues to make that course and speed she is bound to make contact with *Kaiser*,' said the Admiral stonily.

'Sir!' It was the Air Staff Officer. 'The A.O.C. on the line!'

'Thank you,' said the Admiral. 'Tell them to keep trying *Constant*, Hello, S.N.O. here. Listen. . . .'

Rosyth tried *Constant* many times in the next hour. Still there was no reply. The training cruiser, with her crew of cadets and her tiny handful of regulars, her ancient fire-control system and her four old six-inch guns, was somewhere in the North Sea heading south. Across to the west, converging rapidly upon her, was an enemy vessel of vastly superior weight and a broadside of the very latest eleven-inch guns, the ship's company all veterans trained to perfection by the most brilliant officer in the German Navy. . . .

CHAPTER FIFTEEN

Constant, bucking the choppy seas which made her fo'c'sle a very wet and dismal place—she was a bad sea boat—was heading for home and would be glad to get there. She had done her extended cruise. She had been to Shetland.

Harker had got his way. The new class, awaiting at *Ganges* their turn to go to the training cruiser, had been held back, and the normal processes of the training schedule 'frozen' so that *Constant* could take advantage of a movement of the Home Fleet northwards and attach herself to the big ships for the duration of their patrol. Their protection was doubly important as *Constant* was still without radar. With rumours of trouble blowing up in the North Atlantic, *Rutland*, the cruiser due to refit and hand over her radar set to *Constant*, had been retained at the last minute for active duty.

Constant went as far as the Shetland area under the wing of the Home Fleet ships, but here the squadron received a sudden signal to proceed at full speed into the North Atlantic.

There was a scare on. A German raider was out and believed to be making for her home waters by the north-about route.

Constant was detached from the Fleet and Harker was ordered to return to the Firth of Forth immediately. He did not want to go. The captain's indiscreet word in London had told him who the raider might be. The implications of this intelligence were tremendous, the need to stop this German vital. Harker thought that even *Constant* could and should be allowed to help in this desperate hunt. But he had no say in the matter. The Commander-in-Chief wanted no obsolete cruiser with a crew of boys getting in his way, and the old ship retired rather sulkily from a scene of potential death or glory down through the British lake of the North Sea. On her way she met some very ugly weather.

Seasickness laid waste the cadets like a plague. From the Belsen-like horror of the heads an awful chorus of groaning and retching and agonised straining arose where the ashen wretches lay in their vomit. To port, green seas flooded over the side and submerged the guardrails, swirling up waist-high over the green-faced cadavers that clung there. They looked like martyred crows strung up on an allotment or dead soldiers left hanging on the wire after a big push.

They were nearly all, in fact, more dead than alive. But the more astute of the would-be officers realised, even through their misery, that divisional officers were watching them to see whether they would make the attempt to overcome the sickness and take their allotted positions on watch. The pure in heart among them knew that it was their duty to do so, those more venal knew that their chance of gilding their poor matelot's gingerbread with the shining gold of an officer's ring were lessened a great deal if they did not show willing.

Wilsher and Moore were of the sorely afflicted and clung together in their wretchedness under the whaler, spewing in turns over the rail into the awful sea. That they were soaked right through meant less than nothing to them. Their numb hands gripped the rail in something very like rigor mortis. Wilsher was in a worse condition than Moore, but his grip was firmer than the poet's and he knew that in ten minutes' time he must drag himself away from this misery and face the climb up those almost vertical, swaying iron ladders to the bridge. The very thought was extreme agony, but it never occurred to him that he would not do it.

Moore had similar thoughts, but in his mind the call to duty in an hour of suffering was merely a melodramatic dream which was about to happen to somebody else. He longed, dimly and distantly in the back of his subconscious where the poet's lamp still flickered, to see himself doing this heroic thing, to live a poem, but he knew well that he would not do it. The poet still lived in him but the sailor, the real living, doing man, was in his last throes. Bitterly and fiercely Moore, though deathly sick, resented this and loathed himself for it. It could mean, this anger, that he was half-way towards overcoming it . . . but even that thought was only a thought, too rationalised to be a resolution, too much an abstract thing, too much a mere concept. In this way will too much introspective thought bastardise the will, making thought itself a substitute for action, a will to live as brittle as *Constant*'s thin armour. Moore knew this in his bitter, shameful moment of self-knowledge.

Insanely, as thoughts do in moments of physical crisis, he saw across his vision, marching like words on a ticker-tape across the flickering shadows of his mind, the words of Kirkegaard saying: 'The self is that self which constantly relates itself to its own self. . . .' It sounded just like that matelot joke about the bird which, flying in ever-decreasing circles, finally disappeared up its own fundamental orifice. That bird was the intellectual, dying in his own vomit of a physical and spiritual anaemia. Intellectuals never went on watch. They stayed below in their own vomit and dreamed about the world as vomit or shut their eyes and pretended none of it was really happening, that the man with the gun wasn't really there, that the real world did not exist, that the food they ate and the life that allowed them the luxury of being different from other men did not have to be fought for and paid for by their own efforts. Those were the intellectuals, the clever ones, the sneerers. The worst, the intellectually most absurd, become conscientious objectors. The most cowardly and contemptible took up a gun and cried when they found that it was heavy and that there was a man there after all and he had one too and he was pointing it at you and you had to *do* something very quickly or be dead. . . . But whatever they were, they certainly never went on watch.

That's what I am, thought Moore, that wretched thing is what I am. Corduroys and long hair and seasickness are funny jokes and that's what I am. I'm a funny joke in a spot where the crisis calls for a man.

Wilsher was not an intellectual. He would go on watch, in his agony, because if he did not he, and all of life, would cease to move and change and therefore to be. The ship and the self and the sea would disappear in a puff of the wrath of God.

McCutchen, more animal, nearer to the peasant, the eternal simple mind who deludes himself perpetually, is the perpetual underdog and cries for what he can never have forever—the consciousness of life—would go on watch, but there would be no virtue in it for it would require no effort of will, no knowledge of self or of the real meaning of life. In fact he was going round cheerfully now, immune from the sickness, finding out how many dinners he could look forward to today, the eternal scrounger, the wide boy, the picker-up of the honest man's crumbs and the howler for more who has earned none for himself. McCutchen was after the living he felt the world owed him, the gravy the rich always seemed to have....

Wilsher was first up the ladder. Lieutenant-Commander Dickinson noted this without surprise, though it made him want to say 'Good Lad' in his gruff way and tell the wretched young man he had done well. Then he saw to his astonishment that Moore was following him up the slippery rungs. He could not have done it himself, but he could follow where a real man gave him a pattern of life to live by, a pattern that was clear and attractive and logical and made good philosophical sense.

This was the Day of Days for them. If they missed their interview with the captain on the compass platform they knew they could forget about that gold ring on the sleeve. It was no good pleading seasickness. An officer must do his duty at all times, and they wanted to be officers. First McCutchen would go before the captain, then Moore, then Wilsher.

McCutchen was waiting on the bridge when the wretched pair reached there, still green and ill. But the captain was not ready for them yet. His attention was fixed upon another lad.

The masthead lookout, a first-week boy, was in trouble. For the past ten minutes they had been unable to get anything out of him but dismal groans and sound of agonised retching, and when he came down from his eyrie above the main yard he would have a mess to clean up on the flag deck below.

The captain bent to the voicepipe.

'If you are incapable of doing your duty, I shall have to relieve you,' he said loudly. The poor wretch up aloft, swinging in terror through wild parabolas as *Constant* rolled and pitched scarcely heard him, for he was seriously considering hurling himself to the deck below and putting an end to this deathly misery.

The captain turned and saw McCutchen standing confidently beside him.

'Who the devil are you? What do you want?'

'Cadet-rating McCutchen, sir,' said the lad, saluting, 'reporting for captain's interview.'

'Oh,' said the captain, 'yes. Do you think you will make an officer, McCutchen?'

'I think so, sir,' said the cadet.

'H'm. And what sort of ship do you see yourself in when, and if, you are commissioned, McCutchen?'

'M.T.B., sir.'

'Indeed?' The captain raised those wicked eyebrows. 'You have to have a forty-knot brain to drive a forty-knot ship, McCutchen.'

'Yes, sir.'

'You wouldn't want to come back to this ship, then?' The captain asked every cadet this question, mainly for his own amusement. McCutchen had prepared the answer.

'I'd rather go to a *fighting* ship, sir.'

There was a little silence.

'Indeed?' said the captain icily. Even McCutchen realised he had said the wrong thing. Harker glanced aloft. 'So you want some action, my lad?'

'Um, yes, sir.' McCutchen was less certain now, A frosty gleam appeared in the captain's eye.

'You seem to be unaffected by the sickness most incident to cadet-ratings. Are you a good sailor, McCutchen?'

'I ... think so, sir.' A terrible fear, a chill foreboding had clutched at his heart. No, he can't mean that....

'Then get aloft and relieve that wretched lad up there—*at the double!*'

No, he couldn't mean it. McCutchen stared at the captain, struck cold with fear.

'What are you waiting for?' said the captain sharply. 'I said *on the double.*'

'Come on, lad, *move*!' The Chief stepped forward. In a terrible nightmare McCutchen turned and went slowly to the top of the ladder leading down to the flag deck, then began to climb down, his legs shaking, his heart thumping. *I can't do it, I can't do it* beat in his brain with sickening force.

He got to the bottom of the iron rungs, worn to the bright metal by twenty years of matelot boots, and looked upwards. The rungs disappeared up towards the swaying yard and the tiny sentry box in the clouds where he was ordered to go....

I've got to do it, I've got to do it, the others have all done it—all except me. I'm a failure, I'll never be an officer, I'll never be *anything*. I'm a coward, I'll always be a coward, if I don't do this, if I don't climb, *somehow*, up there. I shall always be afraid of everything....

He found, to his amazement, that he had lifted himself on to the bottom rung. He looked up and saw Dickinson watching him stonily from the bridge. Suddenly he thought, I can do it. I mustn't look down or look up, just keep my eyes on the rung ahead and climb. He pulled himself up another rung, his heart beating fast. Suddenly the mast gave a vicious lurch. He closed his eyes, feeling the nausea and the fear begin to rise in him, fighting it off, muttering to himself absurd phrases to drive him on ... 'I'm going to be an officer, I must do it, I must get up there, up aloft, up aloft ...' With a reeling, retching agony of effort he heaved himself on, like a badly wounded man pitifully trying to drag himself along the heaving shell-shocked earth.

Moore and Wilsher watched him and knew what he was suffering. 'Poor old Mac,' said Wilsher. The commander watched the wretched boy struggling like a fly on a flypaper.

'I think he's too far gone,' he said. 'Shouldn't someone else take his place, sir?'

'I'll go up,' said Wilsher.

'I know what you are capable of, Wilsher,' said the captain. 'You've done well to come on watch in your condition, and you, Moore, with your whiskers painted blue. But I *don't* know what that lad up there is capable of and I've got to find out, and this is the only way.'

'If he falls he'll hurt himself badly,' said the commander quietly.

'Then he mustn't fall,' said the captain. 'Have you ever heard of an officer who hasn't got the guts to climb the mast? Do you think we can run a navy with men like that? Do you think we can go out there and beat the Germans with a bunch of lily-white boys like *that*?'

'Excuse me, sir.' Everybody turned round towards the new voice. It was old Jumper.

'Yes?'

'He's really in a bad way, sir,' said the matelot doggedly. 'Look at him clinging on there, sir, he can't go no farther. I've seen that happen many a time, sir. Someone'll have to go and get him down.'

All on the bridge stared at the reeling mast just at the point where the main yard crossed it, where a wretched, panic-stricken figure clung, paralysed with fear, unable either to go farther or to retrace those agonised, bitterly won steps, hung like a robber on a cross, fear and panic crucified on a swaying mast.

'Shall I go and get him down, sir?' asked Jumper in his quiet, hoarse, persistent whisper.

'Very good, Cross, get him down,' said the captain.

Jumper left the bridge and soon they saw him climbing towards the helpless figure of the cadet. He reached the boy and began to try and coax him into retracing his steps to the deck.

It was a full twenty minutes before he succeeded. He led the trembling, white-faced McCutchen, utterly limp and deflated now, forward on to the messdeck.

Now a relief could be sent to the masthead lookout. The boy climbed slowly up the swaying mast and ten minutes later the sick cadet he had relieved was back on deck.

Half an hour had gone by since the wretched McCutchen had first set foot on the ladder of his shame.

It was normal practice to switch off all sending and receiving circuits in the wireless room while a man was climbing the mast, as the passage of live current through the aerials made it dangerous for him.

It was precisely as poor McCutchen had first begun his climb that the Admiralty began its urgent signals to the *Constant*, warning her of the imminent presence of the *Kaiser* and ordering her to alter course and retrace her steps to avoid contact with the pocket battleship. A minute before the training cruiser resumed radio communication the urgent messages ceased temporarily. The Admiralty, with other urgent signals to make to ships in the threatened area, had temporarily abandoned *Constant*.

The new lookout settled himself up aloft and began his search of the horizon. He had been on watch about ten minutes when he sighted smoke on the starboard quarter. Casually, he made his report.

A few minutes later those on the bridge picked up the smoke. No one gave it much thought at first. They had no warning of a ship in the vicinity, but they saw nothing extraordinary about it.

The strange vessel was making good speed, there was no doubt about that. The captain, levelling his glasses on the trailing funnel smoke, estimated that she was making about twenty knots.

He still had his glasses to his eyes when the first parts of the other ship's masts and superstructure came into sight. He saw, above the grey wasteland that lay between the two ships, a distinctive pagoda-shaped bridge tower, then the top of a square, squat funnel . . .

He lowered the glasses, staring in sheer unbelief towards the frowning horizon, the significance of the situation turning his thoughts upside down and making his heart pound.

He heard, from the squawking voicepipe, the sudden, urgent shout of the masthead lookout. With a flash of instinct he covered that blabbing brass mouth with his mittened hand. He did not want anyone but himself to know that he had just been looking at the silhouette of a German pocket battleship.

He could not hope to stifle the facts very long, of course, but he wanted a minute, two minutes to think. By now Dickinson and the Gunner had both turned their glasses on the smoke.

The captain looked quickly from one to the other. Dickinson turned slowly and met his questioning glance with a grim stare.

Then Jan Price lowered his glasses and turned and he saw the same look in his eyes. It was the hard committed look of a man on the brink of battle. . . .

Harker saw the Chief Yeoman watching him. He knew he must make a signal to Admiralty at once. With a jerk of the head he beckoned the Chief.

'Chief, that's a pocket battleship out there,' he said briefly. The young C.P.O.'s eyes widened in astonishment. 'I don't want the cadets to know yet, so go down to the W/T office and tell the duty P.O. to make the signal to Admiralty "Have sighted pocket battleship in position six-o' degrees north, one-degree-four-five east, on course o'-nine-five degrees." '

'Aye aye, sir.' The Chief Yeoman disappeared.

The three officers drew together in the starboard corner of the bridge island.

'It's either *Scheer* or *Kaiser,*' said the Gunner.

'It must be *Kaiser.* It's König breaking for home,' said Dickinson. 'But how in hell did he ever get through?'

'What are we going to do, sir?' said Jan. 'Whatever it is'd better be done pretty sharp. If we've seen her then she'll've seen us by now.'

'She's got radar, Guns,' said Dickinson. He looked at the captain and said, in a voice full of meaning, 'She must have picked us up long ago, sir, decided that with the speed we're making we're no danger to her and kept on her course.'

'Yes, sir,' said Jan. 'She's not interested in us.'

'We can shadow her, sir,' said Dickinson. 'Admiralty will certainly tell us to do that anyway.'

'I don't think we can do that,' said the captain.

He saw the other two look quickly at one another; saw, too, the Chief Yeoman lowering his binoculars and looking towards them, his mouth open in an unbelieving stare. . . .

'If it's the *Kaiser* she's got to be stopped,' said the captain. 'You know that as well as I do.'

'Yes, I know that, sir,' said Dickinson, 'but there's nothing we can do except hold her and keep passing her course and speed to Home Fleet. They must be after her by now.'

'Meanwhile König gets away,' said the captain. The others

heard with alarm the growing note of certainty in his voice. 'You know where our heavy ships are. It will take them hours to reach her. They'll never do it. There's only one thing to do. We must go for her.'

'Do you realise what that means, sir?' said Dickinson.

'It means that we have an outside chance of slowing her down so that the aircraft and the battle-cruisers can overhaul her,' said the captain.

'*Chance,* sir?' said the Gunner. 'We've got no chance, no more'n a snowball's chance in hell, you know that—not against the *Kaiser*!'

'Can we muster guns' crews?' asked Harker.

'We'd have to have the senior class plus a stiffening of the few regular gunners we've got, sir,' said Dickinson.

'We've probably got the legs of her,' said the captain. 'She must be going flat out now. We should be able to make another knot or two without breaking our heart.'

'You can't do it, God in Heaven, you can't do it!' Up until now they had spoken in fierce, stage whispers. Now Dickinson raised his voice angrily. 'This isn't the time for your bloody death or glory destroyer stuff. For God's sake—you have a crew of *boys*! Have you forgotten that? Even with a full compliment of veterans we wouldn't stand the ghost of a chance!'

'That's quite enough!' The captain's voice rose too, ragged and anxious. 'Do you think I don't know all that? Do you think I would send them against *that*,' he flung out an arm and pointed towards the enemy, 'if I didn't know beyond all doubt that it is my duty to do so? We are at war, Dickinson! This is a ship of His Majesty's Navy! It is our duty.'

Duty ... duty ... duty ... it is our duty.... The words sounded like a death knell in Dickinson's mind. Desperately he stared over the salt-caked screen, out across the angry, wave-torn sea towards the heavy menace of the German ship, along the path of duty. It was the same path he had always trodden. Still it lay uphill, strewn still with sharp rocks and the feeble, despairing cries of the dead....

'I realise these are unusual circumstances,' the captain was saying, 'so I am going to do a very unusual thing. You say my ship's company are boys. I say they are men. You imply that they cannot face a fight. I say they can and will. I say it is their duty. I believe they will recognise that it is their duty. I am going to find out. I shall give *them* the choice—to engage the enemy or to hold off and watch him steer for home.'

'But there's no time for that, sir,' said the Gunner incredulously, 'not to muster 'em all, sir. . . .'

'No,' said the captain, 'that will not be necessary.' Swiftly he turned to where Moore was standing, wretched and sick.

'Moore,' he said, 'how would you like to be the conscience of the ship?'

The poet stared at him in astonishment. He's mad, he thought dully. The Chief Yeoman back from the W/T office, heard him too. He's had it, he thought, he's gone round the bend.

'Understand this,' said the captain, speaking levelly and with all the gravity he could bring to bear. 'Out there—and this is not make-believe now—is a German pocket battleship. I think it is our duty to engage her. Normally I would have steered to close her some minutes ago. But this ship, Moore, as you yourself once reminded me, is not a real ship of war. I have no right, it seems, to take her into a one-sided action except with the voluntary agreement of the make-believe sailors who form the bulk of my ship's company. So I am going to put it to you, Moore, as spokesman for all your fellow cadets. The decision is yours, and yours alone—Shall we fight, or shall we let the *Kaiser* go?'

The boy was utterly aghast. Unbelief, then fear, then panic struck him, as he saw with a shock the like of which he had never suffered before, that this was really happening, that the captain meant exactly what he said. For the first time the ugliness of the real world burst in full fury upon his adolescent, self-pitying, self-indulgent little soul. Sick and weary, and now desperately afraid, he bowed under the sudden terrible decision which life, in the words of the captain of the *Constant*, was thrusting on him.

He stared, his eyes wide with fear, at Harker. The captain was smiling. He looked almost gay. Calmly he looked at the boy, waiting for his answer. As every second ticked by the *Kaiser* drew nearer....

His mind shot this way and that, crazily, like a drunkard's. He could think of nothing sane, only ridiculous echoes ... Green to green, red to red, perfect safety, go ahead ... When two ships are crossing so that the one shall have the other on her starboard hand, that one shall give way to the other ... *Give way to the other ... Perfect safety, go ahead* ... Give way to the other ... Give way to the *Kaiser* ... Give way ... give way....

'I'm waiting for your answer, Moore,' the captain's voice broke in harshly from the outside world.

He looked wildly around him. They were all watching him, staring at him, waiting for him to speak. They seemed fixcd, formalised, like figures in an ancient frieze. He gripped the azimuth ring round the top of the compass, hanging desperately to it as something solid and real. It was his boyhood prop and clutch and he clung to it in this testing time before manhood.

'Oh God, oh God,' hc moaned. 'I don't know ... I can't speak for them ... ask them ... ask Wilsher ...'

'I know what Wilsher would say,' said Harker. 'Wilsher is like me. Wilsher is more afraid of failing than he is of that pocket battleship. I *know* what Wilsher and all the Wilshers would say. But I don't know what *you* will say, Moore. I want to know what you are going to do. You represent them all—far more than Wilsher does or I do. I told you, Moore, I am making you the conscience of the ship. What are we going to do? Do we fight or do we turn away? Tell me quickly, lad. We have about one minute left in which to decide to do one thing or the other. After that it may be too late.'

Fight or turn away ... fight or turn away ... way, give way, give way to the other ... give way ... I have always given way ... I shall always give way, always run, never face my fears ... Whether to take up arms ... or by opposing end them ... to be or not to be.... The crazy fragments whirled in his brain, faster and faster to the point of screaming vertigo as the consciousness of the need to say, to do, to *act* whipped them on....

Then, quite suddenly, the mad swirl and agony ceased, faded

right away, leaving something empty, bare and clean, a crystal brightness, like the pellucid clarity after fever or drunken frenzy, when everything is insanely clear and brittle. . . .

To himself he said, I am always running away. I cannot live by running away. Aloud he said, in a steady voice,

'I think we should fight him, sir.'

'Thank you,' said the captain. 'Action Stations.' He bent to the voicepipe.

'Bridge-engine room,' he said sharply. Then came the answering parrot voice through the brass pipe.

'Is that you, Chief? Full speed ahead and, Chief, it's the *Kaiser*. I want everything you've got.'

He straightened up. The action stations alarm was flinging its clangour through the ship. Everywhere men rushed to their posts.

'Dickinson,' said Harker, 'get your guns' crews organised.'

'Aye aye, sir.'

'Mr. Price. . . .' But old Jan had already gone to his action station in the director. 'Bridge-masthead. Come down, lad, you won't be needed up there.' He turned to Moore and Wilsher as the two cadets prepared to rush off the bridge.

'Well, you two,' he started to say, 'this should be the most valuable captain's interview any of you ever had. . . .'

But his last words were lost. There was an unearthly rush of screaming air, a gigantic clap of thunder, a shuddering crash that sent the world reeling. In a flood of panic Moore felt himself hurled right across the bridge to crash against the hard metal. There was a great crashing and splintering and shouting. . . . Quite calmly, he thought: We've been hit. This is the finish.

He got to his feet. He was mildly surprised at how calm he was. There was dust, smoke, wreckage, ruin everywhere. Men were reeling, shouting, moaning, crying. Some were lying still and quiet. . . .

They were still afloat. He noticed, below, the white sheer of the bow wave. They were still making full speed, still on course. He turned and looked aloft.

There was no aloft. There was only a jagged, shattered stump of mast trailing the wreckage of the yard, the lookout, the director and the mortal remains of the men who had manned them . . . there was nothing. On the bridge they were alone, like an island in the sky. On the horizon he saw gunflashes. . . .

'Hard-a-starboard!' It was Dickinson's voice. The captain . . .?

The captain was dead. He lay still in a still, broken heap in the front of the bridge, where a great splinter of white-hot metal had flung his shattered body.

The Gunner had gone too. Old Jan's body, together with those of his director's crew, lay smashed somewhere in the heart of that scattered debris. With them, in that deadly salvo went the master control of *Constant*'s old guns and all her radio aerials. She was utterly alone now on the sea.

Dickinson had the ship. She was his to command now, his to hurl at the German raider in a desperate hope of damaging her in some vital spot, his to turn away from the fight and save five hundred men.

In fact he had no choice. If *Constant* turned away she would still be within range of those eleven-inch guns—in range and even more vulnerable than if she continued to head for the enemy, turning and twisting to avoid his shells, carrying the fight to him with her own guns—when *Kaiser* came within range of the old six-inch—putting her gunners off their stroke, perhaps even scoring a hit or two . . . he had no choice. The dead captain of the *Constant* had already committed them all. A boy had made the decision which was sending them now at twenty-three knots to their deaths. Speaking for all these young men who, five minutes before, had been little more than civilians, he had made the choice to fight. He had chosen like a man, and, like a man, once he has made his bid he must abide by his word and take his punishment.

They had been punished already by *Kaiser*'s first salvo. The German had shot with deadly accuracy, and not a little luck, to shatter with one early shellburst her enemy's director and radio. But her gunners had had plenty of time to aim at leisure and their skill had matured with many months of hard practice.

In spite of the enormous disparity in armament they would

need all their skill. König for once had underestimated his enemy. When his radar had picked up the unknown British ship, she had been doing no more than a harmless fifteen knots and he had put her out of his mind. But when the ship had come within visual contact and he had recognised her to be a cruiser he had had to think a little harder.

But he made another mistake then. He ran over the details of her armament, the solitary gun on her fo'c'sle, the old-fashioned rake of her bows, the ancient bridge structure which had been modern forty years ago, and decided he had nothing to fear from this old wreck. True, she might manage to cap his speed—a pocket battleship had to sacrifice speed in favour of her heavy armament—but the very worst she could possibly do was to shadow him in the traditional role of the light cruiser. It might not be too late even now to cripple her wireless and stop her reporting him.... With this hope in mind he ordered his main armament to open fire. To his delight his crack gunners hit her with their first salvo and brought down her mast. But even if they had missed he would not have worried unduly. The radar screen showed no other ships within dangerous range and it looked as if his daring breakthrough had succeeded. Before any ship could catch him he would be well within reach of home within the sheltering arms of Bergen harbour in Norway. His one worry was aircraft. But this was bad weather for planes. Confident of success he bestrode the parallel of sixty north and steamed towards glory.

Then he saw that the British cruiser was holding her course towards him. She had shaken off her cruel hurt and like an angry terrier was coming in to attack her powerful antagonist. Coolly, her commander was conning her to elude the straddling geysers of spray flung up by *Kaiser*'s shells from the shocked and angry sea. Soon her own guns would be able to open fire.... As long as her engines remained undamaged and her steering under control she could stay with him, and, who knows, a lucky shot...? König was too old a hand to dismiss the possibility of losing everything by the sort of bad luck that so often decided a battle at sea. Other ships must be after him by now, and aircraft. There was no time to lose. He would have to crush her.

But he could not risk that lucky shot getting home. He must open the range again. *Kaiser* turned away to starboard. As she did so her fire slackened, with only her after turret bearing on the British ship.

Dickinson through his glasses saw her turn. The movement confirmed his guess. The German must be very nearly within six-inch range now. He decided to try a shot with the for'ard six-inch. To bring the after guns to bear he would have had to turn *Constant* to unmask her broadside, and that would mean opening the range.

With the gun at maximum elevation *Constant* opened fire for the first time in her life at the enemy.

'Fire!'

Dickinson lowered his glasses as the orange flash and ball of smoke broke from the muzzle of the gun below him, raising them quickly again to his eyes to spot the fall of shot.

Short. Still out of range. But he had made the German turn away off course and cut down her broadside, temporarily by fifty per cent. He saw the triple wink of flashes from her after twelve-inch turret.

'Hard-a-port!'

There was a whistling roar and a wall of white water rose from the sea fine off *Constant*'s starboard bow.

'Starboard ten!'

'Ten of starboard wheel on, sir!' Jumper Cross's hoarse voice came, calm and steady up the voicepipe from the wheelhouse.

Again the eleven-inch shells missed her, pitching this time to port.

Down on the fo'c'sle the gun's crew had gone into quarters firing and Sub-Lieutenant James had come into his own. With Dickinson spotting his fall of shot from the bridge, he was in control of a gun in action at last.

For his gun's crew he had a strange mixture of the old and the very young. His breechworker and gun-captain was a three-badgeman who had joined the Navy within shouting distance of the Boxer Rebellion, his range-taker was a poet of eighteen with a woad-blue chin and his number three was an actor who played

Hamlet like a veteran but who was no veteran on a gun. But they were working together now, too frantically busy to be afraid. Old Jan was dead but he lived on now in the skill he had imparted to his boys. Every round they fired was fired for him. His dead hand guided them.

'Fire!'

The gun belched flame, the breech lunged back. The stripey swung the breech block open, a cadet plunged a new round in, another the charge, a third rammed it home, the breech was closed, the interceptor contact made again....

'Fire!' Moore's voice cracked as he shouted.

Once more the mounting shook and the stink of cordite lay about them.

'Down one hundred!' *They were in range at last.* The last round must have gone *over* the enemy!

'Fire!'

As the gun recoiled this time a great waterfall of spray drenched them. *Kaiser* had turned again, unmasking her whole broadside. She had abandoned the hope of out-distancing the old cruiser. Now she was out to silence her with gunpower. Every few seconds now, six great eleven-inch shells would shriek through the quivering air, seeking out *Constant*'s vital parts, the machinery which gave her power to harry her powerful enemy, the guns which made her dangerous.... And she had to do it quickly. Already this stubborn old ship had lost her priceless time. Already the flickering blips of light had appeared on her radar screen which meant pursuers closing in from the north....

On *Constant*'s fo'c'sle they could hear nothing but the hoarse shouts of the range-taker and the berserk scream and shattering bursts of near misses. Then, over the sound of gunfire they heard a deeper roar. Over their shattered mast, putting them momentarily in cold shadow, came the shapes of wings ... six Royal Air Force Beauforts swept over them, heading straight for the *Kaiser*.

They were the Beauforts from Wick, the first flight of the newly formed squadron which was training there. In fact they had had no time even to begin their training. Their mission was suicidal, but desperately vital. They had to try to hit the German pocket battleship and slow her down. That was the desperate aim of these young men who had never so much as taken off before with a live torpedo under their fuselages. But they carried torpedoes today—the men of the *Constant* saw the silver-blue glint of them in the afternoon sun. . . .

The Admiralty was not concerned with *Constant* now. With one desperate signal from her, then utter silence, they had written her off. The Beauforts which those gallant young volunteers from Coastal Command were steering at this moment low across the heaving sea towards the enemy were there for one purpose only—to hit the *Kaiser*—although to the men aboard the cruiser they looked like rescuing angels.

For one of the young pilots their attack meant precisely that. Peter Price was at the controls of Beaufort 'C' for Charlie, the starboard machine in the thin grey line which roared in low down the barrels of the German guns. He could not know his father was already dead. He only knew he had to go in and get a hit, although he had never once practised dropping a torpedo before. When he heard the call for volunteers and knew that the *Constant* was in the fight, he had been the first to step forward.

As it happened he was the last to make his attack and the only one to made a hit. One by one he saw the others go down before the deadly barrage. A machine would suddenly jerk, stagger, gush with yellow flame, then plunge into the sea and disintegrate. He saw the squadron leader, the last to go, stagger to his feet in the raging furnace of his cockpit. . . . Then the flames hid him from sight and the Beaufort hit the water like a cyclist roaring headlong into a brick wall and the sea put out the flames for ever and swallowed them up.

Then he was alone, flying along the lanes of fiery tracer as if on rails, straight into the mouth of the guns. Miraculously he was still unhit. The top of a gushing jet of spray struck their wing-tip, rocking them wildly. He corrected. Then he was almost upon the German. Funnel and upperworks and the huge slab-sided hull with the spiky crest of gun-flashes filled their vision.

Now! He pressed the toggle. The machine gave an upward

lurch as the heavy torpedo fell away. Unwilling to turn away at once and expose the tender underbelly of the plane to the guns, he held on, roaring over the pocket battleship a matter of inches above her wireless aerials. As he crossed her hull he banked sharply up and away.

On the turn one of *Kaiser*'s guns, elevated to its maximum degree, got him. Suddenly he felt his port wing drop. Looking out along the wing he saw the engine alive with flame. Then he felt a great jolt as the plane was hit again. The nose fell away, the controls went slack and they fell at sickening speed towards the sea. . . . But there had just been time to snatch a glimpse behind and see the tall column of smoke and spray rising from *Kaiser*'s stricken side. . . .

Dickinson saw the hit through his glasses, and saw the dark oil well up from a ruptured tank somewhere inside the *Kaiser*'s split hull. Almost immediately the enemy's speed slowed.

At once Dickinson bent to the voicepipe.

'Port ten!'

He was going to bring her round and bring all *Constant*'s guns to bear. This was the moment to try, when the enemy was badly hit and slowed and in confusion.

But the cruiser's guns never got their broadside off. As she turned to port to unmask them, *Constant* turned straight into a full salvo from *Kaiser*'s main armament. At least four eleven-inch shells struck her hull and upperworks simultaneously and burst in a terrible welter of destruction.

The cruiser lurched and rolled like a beaten fighter, the whole of her superstructure shrouded in smoke. Then, as she came upright again, great flames, like vicious beasts bounding from their hiding places, leapt out of the shattered, yawning chasms torn in her plates and decks and gun-platforms. The flames leapt, writhed and danced, then swept together with a hoarse crackle and roar as they ate ravenously into wood and paint-work. In a moment the whole ship, from her bridge down her whole length, hiding the twisted stumps of her funnels, the mangled heaps of metal that had been her guns, was burning. The fire was the funeral pyre of a hundred men and boys.

But out of the heart of the fire gouts of black smoke drifted from her boilers. The smoke spilled out of huge holes in the decks where there had once been funnels and drifted aft, slipping and sliding suddenly here and there in the fiery, rushing air. *Constant* was still under command, still making her way through the water, and from the isolated plateau of her fo'c'sle came the flash and bark of the one gun left in action. Another smashing salvo merely straddled her this time as the faithful hands of Jumper Cross on the wheel turned her out of the line of fire, so that their only effect was to drench her shattered decks with tons of spray and put out much of the fire their predecessors had started. With the hiss of the fire quenched to steam came the terrible sounds of mingled screams and shouts and inhuman, animal keening....

Those left alive knew now that it was only a question of time before the ship sank and took them all with her. But still the men in the engine and boiler-rooms held on and kept her on course through the shell-shocked sea, toiling in semi-darkness now, in lurid flame-lit darkness and the white curtain of escaping steam, their only guide the intolerable sounds that crept down the voicepipes from above. It was a miracle none of those shells had hit a magazine, or the ship would have gone in one great flash of light.

Still the single six-inch on the fo'c'sle, her barrel red-hot, continued to fire and spit her anger at the enemy. They were firing over open sights now, James controlling the fire. All electrical circuits had gone and each round was fired mechanically.

But they knew they had only a short time to live. Dully they watched two great columns of boiling white spray spring up in a line pointing straight at the ship.

The third of that bunch, they knew, must come inboard.

It burst full on the bridge and all but obliterated the *Constant*'s last surviving pocket of resistance.

Dickinson was facing to starboard, glasses to his eyes, when the salvo landed. He was conscious only of a great blow which flung him sideways against the front screens of the bridge, then he knew no more.

Presently, by the throbbing, terrible pain in his head, he knew he was still alive. Slowly he felt about him, groping for some firm purchase. But nothing seemed the same. The air rushed coldly about him and he could hear the crackling of fire and the hoarse shouting of a distant voice.

He thought, *I must open my eyes, I can't open my eyes*. He could not seem to open his eyes. Then he felt with his hands and felt clumsily over his face and knew that they were open. But they were full of blood and pain and darkness.

He lowered his hands. He felt himself sobbing. *No,* he thought, I mustn't give way. He heard a soft, wounded voice from far away saying, 'You should have taken more care of them.' *The ship,* he thought, *the ship, I must get her out of this, I must get her away.*

He groped around him again and presently he found what he thought must be the canted remains of the binnacle. Slowly, painfully, grimly he hauled himself to his feet. It was all silent round him, save for that strident, hoarse voice calling urgently again and again from the distance....

'Is anyone there?' His own voice was remote and unreal to him. There was no answer. He knew then that all on the bridge were dead. He knew by the sway and tremor of the deck beneath him that the ship was still making way through the water, so they must be all right below decks still.

Still the hoarse, insistent voice called faintly from the black outer world around him. Suddenly he realised that it came from the voicepipe. With a few stumbling movements he found it. The mouthpiece was jagged and he tore his hand on it. Bending down he heard the quartermaster's anxious urgent voice say, 'Are you all right? Wheelhouse-bridge, are you all right?'

'Bridge-wheelhouse,' he said weakly in that unreal, distant voice.

'Thank God it's you, sir,' said Cross. 'I thought you must have all had it.'

'I'm all right,' said Dickinson. 'But I think ... everyone else up here is gone ... how are things down there?'

'Oh, we're okay, sir,' said the leading hand. 'We're still on course o'-nine-o' degrees, sir.'

'Does she answer the wheel?'

'Yes, I think the steering's okay, sir.'

'All right. Starboard twenty then. We're getting out of here.'

'Starboard twenty, sir. . . . Twenty of starboard wheel on, sir,' called the strong, cheerful voice that seemed to come from a distant world of sunshine and light.

'Steady.'

'Steady, sir . . . course two-six-eight degrees, sir.'

'Steer two-seven-o' degrees.'

'Steer two-seven-o' degrees, sir.'

It was guesswork. They didn't know it below but it was guesswork.

'What about the men on the fo'c'sle?'

'They're okay, sir. A bit chokka, I reckon, now the *Kaiser*'s out of range,' said Cross. He thought it was funny that Dickinson should ask that. Couldn't he see for himself? The poor bastard must be hurt. . . .

'What is the *Kaiser* doing? Why has she stopped firing?'

What is the Kaiser doing? Why. . . . Oh, my God! He can't see . . . he's. . . .

'Here, son,' said Jumper, 'take the wheel. Course two-seven-o' degrees. I'm going up to the bridge.'

On his way out of the wheelhouse he bumped into one of the signalmen and the P.O. Telegraphist. Glancing along the main deck aft he could see the small parties of men in twos and threes groping their way among the ruin of the superstructure, looking for the wounded.

He said, 'I'm going on the bridge. Dickinson's alive and I think he's blinded. Come on.'

It took them a long time to climb to the shattered bridge island.

There they found Dickinson, propped up against the binnacle. His face was streaming blood and his sightless eyes stared out over the sea.

He heard them picking their way towards him. He said, lifting one hand from the torn mouth of the voicepipe,

'I seem to have cut my hand.'

'Don't worry, sir,' said the leading hand. 'We've got things under control.'

'What is *Kaiser* doing?' asked Dickinson.

'Oh, she's legging for home, trailing enough oil to lead our blokes straight to her, sir.'

'She'll get away after all,' said the officer.

'Oh, I don't think she'll get far, sir. The last round they fired from "A" gun, sir, just before we caught this last packet, hit the Jerry smack on her bridge, sir. They went round in circles for a bit, till they got her under control again. I don't reckon many of 'em could have got out of that bridge alive, sir.'

'Good,' said Dickinson. 'Good. Fall them out, will you, and ask Sub-Lieutenant James to come to the bridge.'

'Aye aye, sir. And how about you, sir?'

'Afterwards,' said Dickinson, 'afterwards.'

'I'll send someone up to see to you, sir,' said the leading hand.

When James finally gained the shattered wasteland of the compass platform he found the lieutenant-commander standing, tall and calm, among its ruins, as if waiting patiently for him.

'Who is that?' he said.

'James, sir,' said the subby, wonderingly.

'Oh, James, good,' said Dickinson. 'I want you to take over here and get us home. I am afraid I can't see. . . .'

Later someone came and bound his eyes up and the two men, the young and the old, stayed together on the bridge of the shattered cruiser, nursing her home.

When the first wave of bombers from the carrier flew over the scene of action they saw two ships. At masthead height they roared over the twisted, distorted decks of an old cruiser who had just fought her last and only fight. From her fo'c'sle a small group of men at her only remaining gun waved at the aircraft. Half of them had white bands round their arms, one pilot noticed. They would be some of the cadets. Plucky young bastards. From the almost unrecognisable bridge first one, a young, jaunty-looking figure, then the other, an older officer with a white bandage round his head, waved as well.

Then the planes went on, flying down to the oil slick to the distant horizon. Hull down on the pale edge of the sea they picked up the limping shape of the *Kaiser*. They attacked and put four torpedoes into her so that she lay stopped in the water. Two hours later the heavy ships of the Home Fleet came up with her and sent her to the bottom. The few survivors told them that König was dead, killed by the solitary shellburst from *Constant* which had shattered his bridge.

Constant was a survivor. Fiercely she staggered home, clinging to life, burning and broken. Her dead and wounded lay within her; some, both dead and injured, trapped inextricably in the twisted, blackened wreck of her upper deck, others lying below in the fever and ugliness of pain.

Those uninjured or with light wounds helped to ease the anguish of others. Here and there about the ship was a man with his head bandaged kneeling by the side of a badly wounded messmate, or a grim-faced seaman covering the face of another. Men from below came up to see what had happened to their ship and to help those on the upper deck. They blinked in the bleak sunshine, then stared about them, shocked, at the smoking ruins. Occasionally a man would sink to the deck, utterly exhausted or suddenly overcome by shock, and half-lie, half-sit where he had collapsed, his head sunk upon his chest.

One of these was Moore. He was unhurt, untouched by fire or blast or flying metal, but he had taken quite enough punishment. Oddly, he could not remember much of the fighting. It only occurred to him later that it had been his decision which had brought about this holocaust, and the fact that he had said the words which sank the *Kaiser* and blew the dream of König to pieces never entered his stunned mind.

He could not remember that they had fought a great enemy ship and won. The battle did not seem to matter now.

And on the shattered bridge a blinded veteran and a pink-cheeked boy officer brought the ship home.

Dickinson would not leave his post, even when destroyers came alongside and took the rest of the wounded off. The two of them stayed on the bridge until *Constant,* still under her own steam, made port.

When she steamed slowly in, every ship in the anchorage saluted her. Men cheered and sirens boomed all along the lines of ships. She had no funnels or upperworks left, only the remains of a bridge and a solitary gun. But the gun was trained fore-and-aft and there were two lines of men on her fo'c'sle. H.M.S. *Constant* was still under command, still making way through the water.

THE END

Science Fiction

☐ 552 08499 9 REACH FOR TOMORROW *Arthur C. Clarke* 5/–
☐ 552 08516 2 NEW WRITINGS IN S.F. 17 *John Carnell* 5/–
☐ 552 08453 0 DRAGONFLIGHT *Anne McCaffrey* 5/–
☐ 552 08401 8 A CANTICLE FOR LEIBOWTIZ *Walter M. Miller Jr.* 6/–
☐ 552 08478 6 LOGAN'S RUN *William F. Nolan & George Clayton-Johnson* 4/–
☐ 552 08500 6 THE INNER LANDSCAPE *Peake Ballard Aldiss* 5/–
☐ 552 08461 1 THE ALIENS AMONG US *James White* 5/–

General

☐ 552 98434 5 GOODBYE BABY AND AMEN *David Bailey & Peter Evans* 25/–
☐ 552 07566 3 SEXUAL LIFE IN ENGLAND *Dr. Ivan Bloch* 9/6
☐ 552 08403 4 LIFE IN THE WORLD UNSEEN *Anthony Borgia* 5/–
☐ 552 08432 8 PUT-OFFS AND COME-ONS *A. H. Chapman, M.D.* 5/–
☐ 552 07593 0 UNMARRIED LOVE *Dr. Eustace Chesser* 5/–
☐ 552 07950 2 SEXUAL BEHAVIOUR *Dr. Eustace Chesser* 5/–
☐ 552 08402 6 SEX AND THE MARRIED WOMAN *Dr. Eustace Chesser* 7/–
☐ 552 07400 4 MY LIFE AND LOVES *Frank Harris* 13/–
☐ 552 98121 4 FIVE GIRLS (illustrated) *Sam Haskins* 21/–
☐ 552 97745 4 COWBOY KATE (illustrated) *Sam Haskins* 21/–
☐ 552 98307 1 NOVEMBER GIRL (illustrated) *Sam Haskins* 21/–
☐ 552 08362 3 A DOCTOR SPEAKS ON SEXUAL EXPRESSION IN MARRIAGE *Donald W. Hastings M.D.* 10/–
☐ 552 98247 4 THE HISTORY OF THE NUDE IN PHOTOGRAPHY (illustrated) *Peter Lacey and Anthony La Rotonda* 25/–
☐ 552 98345 4 THE ARTIST AND THE NUDE (illustrated) 21/–
☐ 552 08069 1 THE OTHER VICTORIANS *Steven Marcus* 10/–
☐ 552 08010 1 THE NAKED APE *Desmond Morris* 6/–
☐ 552 07965 0 SOHO NIGHT AND DAY (illustrated) *Norman and Bernard* 7/6
☐ 552 08105 1 BEYOND THE TENTH *T. Lobsang Rampa* 5/–
☐ 552 08228 7 WOMAN: a Biological Study *Philip Rhodes* 5/–
☐ 552 98178 8 THE YELLOW STAR (illustrated) *Gerhard Schoenberner* 21/–
☐ 552 08456 5 COMPLETE BOOK OF JUKADO SELF-DEFENCE (illustrated) *Bruce Tegner* 6/–
☐ 552 07918 9 BRUCE TEGNER'S COMPLETE BOOK OF KARATE 6/–
☐ 552 98479 5 MADEMOISELLE 1 + 1 *Marcel Veronese & Jean-Claude Peretz* 21/–

Western

☐ 552 07756 9 SUDDEN—TROUBLESHOOTER *Frederick H. Christian* 4/–
☐ 552 08451 4 THE OWLHOOT *J. T. Edson* 4/–
☐ 552 08400 X THE RIO HONDO WAR *J. T. Edson* 4/–
☐ 552 08262 7 BUTCH CASSIDY AND THE SUNDANCE KID *William Goldman* 4/–
☐ 552 08270 8 MACKENNA'S GOLD *Will Henry* 4/–
☐ 552 08475 1 NO SURVIVORS *Will Henry* 5/–
☐ 522 08514 6 ALIAS BUTCH CASSIDY *Will Henry* 4/–
☐ 552 08485 9 THE FAST FIRST DRAW *Louis L'Amour* 4/–
☐ 552 08476 X GALLOWAY *Louis L'Amour* 4/–
☐ 552 08484 0 GUNS OF TIMBERLAND *Louis L'Amour* 4/–

Crime

☐ 552 08473 5 SCANDAL AT HIGH CHIMNEYS *John Dickson Carr* 4/–
☐ 552 08498 0 WARN THE BARON *John Creasey* 4/–
☐ 552 08316 X FOUNDER MEMBER *John Gardner* 5/–
☐ 552 08513 8 A COOL DAY FOR KILLING *William Haggard* 4/–
☐ 552 08472 7 THE INNOCENT BYSTANDERS *James Munro* 5/–
☐ 552 08449 2 I'M TRYING TO GIVE IT UP *Desmond Skirrow* 5/–
☐ 552 08520 0 KISS ME DEADLY *Mickey Spillane* 4/–
☐ 552 08425 5 THE SHADOW GAME *Michael Underwood* 4/–

All these books are available at your book shop or newsagent: or can be ordered direct from the publisher. Just tick the titles you want and fill in the form below.

CORGI BOOKS. Cash Sales Department, P.O. Box 11, Falmouth, Cornwall.
Please send cheque or postal order. No currency, and allow 6d. per book to cover the cost of postage and packing in U.K., 9d. per copy overseas.

NAME ....

ADDRESS ....

(SEPT '70) ....